Second Chances

Elissa Daye

This is a work of fiction. Names, characters, places, and incidents are products of the author's imagination or are used fictitiously and are not to be construed as real. Any resemblance to actual events, locations, organizations, or persons, living or dead, is entirely coincidental.

World Castle Publishing, LLC
Pensacola, Florida
Copyright © Elissa Daye 2019
Paperback ISBN: 9781950890668
eBook ISBN: 9781950890675
First Edition World Castle Publishing, LLC, October 7, 2019
http://www.worldcastlepublishing.com
Licensing Notes
Cover: Melissa Davis
Editor: Maxine Bringenberg

Chapter 1

The bell jingled when Caydence stepped through the door, and she was reminded how literal it was. Bells jingling over the door of a bridal shop, like the proverbial wedding bells that would hang on the back of the limousine the day she married Dalton. Just thinking about becoming Mrs. Dalton Mills made her heart flutter. Two more months, and Caydence would finally say I do. At twenty-eight she was more than ready.

"Miss Lawson?" The bridal attendant came rushing over to meet with her.

"Good afternoon. I was told I could try on my dress today?" Caydence was starting to feel a little nervous. What if it looked hideous? She had given in to Dalton when he requested they use one of the wedding planners that was well-known in his new social circle. Caydence wanted a simple gown, one that twirled like a flower around her. She had always wanted a small outdoor wedding somewhere like a vineyard, or even a beach. Having the wedding at one of the most expensive chateaus had never been on her radar. It was

3

going to be a stuffy affair that would feel more like a business event than her own wedding, but Caydence was learning to let that go.

"Yes, of course. We were expecting you. Rosalind confirmed with us earlier. She asked us to take pictures for her."

Great. Highest paid wedding planner in their city, and she couldn't be bothered to show up for the fitting. The woman literally got paid to tell her what to do. That did not seem like a fair exchange to her, but Dalton always waved her concerns away because, after all, what else did Caydence have to do with her time? He did not acknowledge her full time blogging as a career, even though she made good money doing it. Caydence tried not to let that get to her, because she could continue to work from home when they started a family. She sure hoped that would be sooner rather than later. Caydence wanted to be young enough to chase her kids around without getting out of breath.

As she followed the woman to the changing room, Caydence saw the large puffy tulle pushing against the confines of the lace and silk. It looked as trapped as she was going to feel the minute she put the dress on. She tried to shake the thoughts from her head. This should have been one of the most wonderful moments in her life. Instead, she felt like an afterthought in her own wedding. She loved Dalton, though, so she would do this for him.

She quickly undressed to her under things and let the woman assist her as she stepped into the huge, poofy gown. Something unexpected happened. The minute the gown was zipped up, Caydence felt a smile forming at the corners of her mouth. While it would not have been her first choice, she was surprised to see that the dress actually fit her quite well. It was the most extravagant thing she had ever worn in her life. The bodice was bejeweled and glistened when she moved her body from left to right. The top fit her like a glove, enhancing her breasts without making her look too top heavy. Caydence was well endowed, and she did not want to display her girls when she walked down the aisle.

When she was done dressing, the blonde associate led her out of the changing room and into the viewing room, which had mirrors on all sides. She helped Caydence onto the small pedestal in the middle and stood back to admire her work. "What do you think, Miss Lawson?"

"It's beautiful," Caydence answered her. And it was, even the yards upon yards of material that made her bottom half look like some cloudy marshmallow. She started to nibble on her lip as she thought about how hard it was going to be to walk in this thing.

"But?" It was as if the woman could sense her dilemma.

"Not quite my style." Caydence smoothed down some of the fabric in front of her. "It kind of makes me feel like a French poodle at a dog show."

"You look beautiful in it though."

"Do I?" Caydence tilted her head left and right, trying to make up her mind how she felt.

"Rosalind has good taste."

"You're right." That must mean Caydence had horrible taste. She let out a slow sigh and looked down at the floor.

How was she ever going to make Dalton a proper wife if the finer things just made her feel like the kid who got caught picking her nose? His work functions took up a lot of their time whenever they were together. Caydence always felt like she was on duty when she spent time with him. At least when they were married, she would be able to spend more time with the man she had fallen in love with, and not the one who was putting on a show for the rest of the world.

"Let's add a few things for the full effect," offered the brunette who had walked over to assist them. When she returned, the woman put some clip on earrings over Caydence's ear lobes, and pulled her hair up with a clip. Then she placed a sparking tiara on top of her head with a veil that had several jewels sewn onto it to make it shimmer in the right light. The combination of pearls and faux diamonds around her neck made the look complete.

Caydence gasped aloud. "I look like a princess."

"You sure do." The first woman looked to her assistant in relief. "Shall I take the pictures now?"

"Sure." Caydence stood before them and posed when they asked her to, even offering up a feeble smile.

"Looks like the fit is perfect. I'll let Rosalind know. We usually keep them here for our clients, and she will pick it up a few days before. Where is the wedding?"

"Red Orchard Chateau," answered Caydence.

"Oh! That's hard to get. Good for you!" The brunette almost squealed.

Yes, good for her. Caydence tried not to roll her eyes. It wasn't marrying him that made her feel the dread she had—

it was the whole process of getting there. She was willing to make these concessions, if only to help move their relationship along.

Their engagement had lasted three years already, with a few missteps here and there. First, Caydence had been needed to take care of her ailing grandmother. While she was away, he had poured himself into his work, so much so that it had taken up most of his time. Dalton had been so possessed with his work over the past few years, trying to earn the atta boy he thought he deserved, that he had pushed their plans to the side. Caydence had almost given up after year two, but then he had made junior partner at his company. That had put their relationship back on track, for the partners were family men, which inspired him to finally make the move. A year ago today, actually — that was when they'd finally set the date.

She was ushered back into the dressing room and started to get undressed. The same process as the dressing, only backwards. She was not thrilled to be half naked in front of strangers, but she had no choice. Not really. This was just the way it was, right? Caydence would have been happy eloping at this point in time. She was tired of them living separate lives. While he spent most of his week in the city, Caydence was in her condo a few hours away. Soon, she would no longer just have weekends with him, she would have forever. Caydence was more than ready to move forward.

As she left the room, she waved to the two women. "Thank you."

Now that she was done with that, she decided to surprise

Dalton. He had told her earlier he was working at the office all day when she had asked him to have lunch with her. It wasn't often that Caydence was in the city with him at the same time. She could at least pop in to say hello, give him a shoulder massage — or something else if he were lucky.

Caydence smiled wickedly. The thought of doing something naughty…well, that usually wasn't her style. He often complained that he wished she were more impulsive. That was something she would be happy to change. As she hopped in her car, she started to think about what she could get away with in the light of day. It had been a long time since they'd had sex. In fact, now that she thought about it, Caydence could not remember when the last time was. Hard to be impulsive when it was a non-existent situation. Dalton worked so hard that he was often too tired by the time he was done. She would have to endeavor to change that.

Typing in his office address, she followed the directions to his office and put some music on that would take the doldrums away. By the time she pulled into his office parking lot, Caydence was already trying to think of something clever to say to him the minute she saw him.

It only took her a few minutes to get to the top floor, even though the time in the elevator felt like forever. When the doors slid open, she adjusted her top and did a once over before exiting the elevator. Caydence walked over to the secretary's desk but did not see her there. She stood there wondering what she should do. Normally, if she wanted to talk to Dalton during the day, she would call the secretary and she would buzz her through if he was available.

He was supposed to be in the office all day today. Caydence nibbled her lip. She knew he would be surprised to see her, but she also didn't want to interrupt him. What if she just listened at the door first, to make sure he wasn't in a meeting? It seemed reasonable to her. Walking to the door, she listened to see if she heard voices. When she didn't hear a thing, she decided to take a chance.

Opening the door, Caydence went to greet him with a smile, but the words were caught in a gasp. Oh yes, Dalton was working all day. Apparently, working his secretary over would have been a better description. His hands squeezed her behind as she rode him on top of the black leather couch. She was almost impressed at his stamina, and the fact that neither one of their bodies was sliding down the slippery leather.

"Eh hem," she interrupted them. "You forgot to lock the door."

"Shit! Caydence.... I can explain...."

"No. I got the picture just fine." Sliding the diamond ring off her finger, she walked over to his desk. She winced as it plinked down on the glass top and tears started to fill her eyes. "I assume you can talk to Rosalind?"

"Wait, Caydence. We can work this out...," he sputtered, pushing his secretary off his lap.

"Oh, no, no. Don't stop on my account. You can have him. I'm done wasting my time." Caydence slammed the door on the way out.

When one of the partners smiled at her as she was leaving, she tried to rein in her emotions. She was not one to make a scene, but apparently, she was too easy to see through.

"Everything okay, Miss Lawson?"

The devil on her shoulder told her to lead him to the other room, but Caydence didn't have to. Both her fiancé and his secretary were now visible, as Dalton had tried to follow her. "Peachy. It was nice knowing you."

"What is going on here, Mills?" His face was already starting to turn red. "Get yourself in order and meet me in my office at once."

Dalton sputtered slightly. "Yes, sir."

When Caydence met Dalton's eyes, his expression was accusatory. It was as if he thought if she had not come to visit, this would not have happened. Oh, she was sure it would have. If not today, another. Clearly he was careless and self-absorbed. As she walked away, she couldn't help wondering how in the hell she had gotten to this point. Three years of her life wasted on a man who clearly only wanted her to be on his arm to show off. An item to own, not one to cherish or put any time or effort into.

The tears fell as soon as the elevator doors closed. Caydence was a puddle of a mess by the time she got to the bottom floor. She almost bumped into a man entering just as she exited. "I'm so sorry."

"Are you all right?" His voice was nice enough, but Caydence did not look up.

"No...yes." Caydence didn't know how to answer the question. Her anger tried to override her pain, but they were both mingling together in discord.

"Here." He offered her a tissue that he pulled from one of his pockets, but she warded his hand away.

"I'm fine. Thank you."

She sniffed slightly, but continued on her way. Caydence just wanted to get home, where she could curl up with a pint of ice cream and cry until her tear ducts no longer worked. Just when she was starting to get used to the idea of looking like a pasty piñata, now she had to figure out what to do with the rest of her life.

As she left the door, she never saw the gentleman watching her leave. He walked over to the front desk. "Do you know who that was?"

Chapter 2

The last two months had been living hell for Caydence. As much as she had wanted to put the whole thing behind her, the more she looked around her, the more she realized that her entire house was filled with things that reminded her of the one man who had wasted all her time. She wanted to have a bonfire on her lawn, purging all his things from her life, but there was a city ordinance that prevented her from doing so, unfortunately.

Days passed slowly, and Caydence pushed herself back into her work, trying to ignore the walking zombie state she had fallen into. Food no longer tasted good to her. It was bland, just like the rest of her life. Nothing excited her, not even the work that had sustained her just a few months ago. Yet she barreled, existing, not really living, as she tried to figure out just where it had all gone wrong. Was she so emotionally defunct that Dalton had to find what he needed in someone else's arms? What about what she had needed? Had that ever really mattered?

Taking a deep breath, Caydence considered what would

make her feel better, especially today of all days. At this precise moment, if everything had gone to Rosalind's schedule, she would be walking down the aisle to the man she had thought she would spend the rest of her life with. She had never known he was spending most of it in other women's beds. She was pretty sure there was more than one, but she didn't have the proof to make that theory substantial. Once a cheater, always a cheater. She almost felt sorry for whichever woman fell for his charming smile next. Maybe they were using him for the same exact thing, but she didn't know how. He was really a one trick pony where sex was concerned. Or was that just the way he was with her? Had she been that boring?

Letting out an irritated sigh, Caydence turned on the song she was intended to walk down the aisle to and smiled at the irony. A funeral dirge would have been more appropriate. As with everything else that had plagued her since the day she left, here was the biggest reminder staring her in the face. The dress from hell. As the music chimed over her speakers, she gripped the scissors in her hand. Not caring how much the dress must have cost, or what it was supposed to signify, she started to plunge the metal into the folds upon folds of material.

"A chain saw might have been easier," she said wryly. "Ah well."

A satisfied smile filled her face as the jewels started to fall down on the floor around her. She had truly hated those things. The fact that Dalton had never understood what she wanted or even tried to make her happy just continued to grate on her nerves. She tossed the scissors to the floor and started to rip the fabric with her hands. When a loud rip resulted, she smiled. She counted down the minutes as she continued to annihilate the ghastly beast, and saw the irony in the fact that the last rip happened right when the ceremony would have been over.

Was it wasteful? Perhaps. But Caydence deserved the release that came when she looked around her at the disarray on the floor. Like a cloud of downy angst it lay there, the last remnants of all the promises that had been broken over the years. Two months might not be enough to heal the heartache, but it was a start.

Dalton had tried to contact her, but she had nothing left to say to the man. The dress was just one example at how angry she was right now. She was fairly certain she would throw the sharpest object at him if she saw him face to face. He had not even been man enough to try, the coward. Especially considering how he had tried to blame her for him almost losing his job. Apparently, he was in a fair amount of trouble for having an affair during work hours. Not to mention the fact that everything he had done violated the sexual harassment policy from human resources. Not like it was hard to figure out that he shouldn't be banging his secretary on company grounds, or anywhere for that matter, but sure, go ahead and blame her for it. Just like everything else in their failing relationship.

Nothing she had done was ever good enough. Caydence had not realized this at the time. He had an ego the size of Texas, thinking that he deserved the finer things in life. She had no idea he was trying to change her to fit his idea of what was acceptable for his agenda. He really was a jackass. If her father had been alive, he would have told her to dump the ignorant fool a long time ago. That was the thing, though—everyone she loved was gone, and Dalton had fed into that loneliness, whether intentionally or not. Caydence had always seen him in a much different light. It's funny the way things change the minute someone breaks your heart.

Caydence sighed. After today, she would try not to think about what could have been. Even though she knew she would still think about it, she should at least try. That was why she had decided to keep her reservation for the cruise she had booked almost a year ago. It was the only thing that Dalton had let her have control over. When she had received the confirmation reminder for the two week cruise that they were supposed to go on, Caydence was so run down from dealing with everything that she made the decision to put the cruise to good use. One of them should get some use out of it. She was pretty sure Dalton wouldn't show his face anywhere near it. Caydence had made herself pretty clear that she didn't want anything to do with that man any more.

So Caydence put her efforts into planning to enjoy every moment she was away. She had already put in for time away with the various clients she blogged for, creating their content for the two weeks well ahead of time so that it would post while she was on vacation. This would be the first real vacation she'd had in over five years. Tomorrow was the day.

"Hmmm...now what to do?"

Caydence looked down at the dress again. Pity. She almost wished she could frame it as some kind of pop art, but that would probably take too much effort. She went to retrieve a garbage bag and started to pile the pieces into it.

"Guess I should have brought three bags in," she muttered to herself before turning back to get more. By the time she was done, there were four puffy black garbage bags filled with the remnants of a future she was glad she no longer had to be a part of.

Yawning, Caydence realized that she was going to have to go to bed early if she were going to make it to the airport in time for the flight that would bring her to the city closest to port. Thankfully, the cruise line had a shuttle from the airport to where the ship was docked. Her bags were already packed and ready to go. All she needed now was to go sleep.

***

The next morning, Caydence woke up with the alarm with a smile on her face. Time for some fun in the sun. Her drive to the airport was uneventful. Even checking in for her flight seemed to go perfectly. It was shaping up to be a wonderful day. When she finally made it to the dock, she started to feel the first wave of excitement.

As Caydence made her way up the walkway, she saw the large cruise ship as it loomed over the dock. Even though she had read how large the ship was with its seemingly infinite decks, she'd had no idea how humongous it actually was.

The wind nearly knocked the hat off her head, and she quickly put her hand on top of it. "Goodness."

"Awfully windy today," commented an older lady in line in front of her.

"I guess it is."

"Is your husband already on board?" The woman asked her curiously.

The gentleman at her side interrupted her. "Marianne, that's not polite."

"Well, it is a couple's cruise. Not one of those hook up ones." Marianne held her hand up near her mouth. "That's where I met Eddie."

Eddie winked at Caydence. "Best vacation ever."

"Says you. I think I spent most of my week sick in my cabin."

"I don't think you were sick, if I remember correctly."

Marianne blushed slightly. "Oh dear, you're right."

"Hope you have as many happy years as we have," Eddie wished her.

Caydence did not know what to say. "How long have you been married?"

"Ten years," Marianne answered almost wistfully. "He's my second chance."

"Mine too. Life's too short. You can't live with regrets."

Preach, she wanted to say. She had already been learning that lesson, loud and clear. "Good for you."

"You're never too old to feel young in love." Marianne grabbed Eddie's hand and squeezed it.

"Looks like we're moving," Caydence pointed out. She was thankful for that. Caydence was starting to feel a little awkward. If this was what she would be in for the entire time, the cruise was going to feel like eternity. She had forgotten that this was a couple's cruise and that she had booked the honeymoon suite. Closing her eyes, she tried to maintain a carefree composure. She had gone past the heartbreak, most of it at least. Now that she was firmly into the anger portion of her healing, Caydence was starting to feel a little stronger.

Caydence walked over to the check-in terminal and pulled out all her proper papers. "Hello. Caydence Lawson."

"Welcome aboard, Ms. Lawson." The clerk checked over her information and started to look her up in the system. "Or should I say, Mrs.? Congratulations! I see you have the honeymoon suite."

"Yes...." She was about to correct him, but then she wondered what the point was. It was less than likely that she would have any further interaction with him.

"Here are your key cards. Looks like there's already been one issued."

What did that mean? Caydence just brushed it off. Probably nothing. "Thank you."

"This card gives you access to your room and any of the amenities you have attached to your account. If you purchase anything in the gift shops, that will be charged to your account. Incidentals will be charged as well. Soda and food are included on your plan, but alcohol is extra. Just use this card and it will be charged to your card on file." The man continued on with the same explanation he must give to everyone who stopped to check in. He handed her the plastic card that she would use to get into her room and use anywhere along the ship.

"Thank you."

"My pleasure. Here is your itinerary and a map. There are also a few spare maps in your room, just in case you misplace it. Your bags should already be in your room."

"Great." Everything seemed to be going flawlessly so far. Now she could just relax, something she had not done in quite some time.

"If you have any questions, requests, or concerns, please call this number here from the line inside your room. We hope you have a fantastic stay."

"Thank you.

Caydence looked at the map and went to look for her room, where hopefully her luggage would already be. She was thankful they had that service; while she had packed light, the idea of lugging her things down the hallway was not something she looked forward to. She sighed in relief when she finally found her door. Time to finally spend some time on herself. Two weeks of uninterrupted silence from the rest of the world. No more sad phone calls from her parents, no friends trying to make her come out of her house. This was time just for her.

Chapter 3

As she neared her door, she took a deep breath. This was it. A quiet room, hopefully with a fantastic view. She slid the card in the slot and waited for the click. Opening the door, she heard a voice call out.

"Occupied."

"What do you mean, occupied? Who the hell are you?" Caydence put her hands on her hips and shook her head at the man sitting on the bed before her. She knew this was her room; it had been listed on the reservations the minute she had selected it. How could he possibly have the same room?

"My secretary got the tickets for me. Not sure of the exact details, except that the man selling his ticket was anxious to part with it."

"Secretary?" How in the hell had this man gotten Dalton's ticket? And why would he sell it? Hadn't he already taken enough? Asshole. Caydence was ready to scream. If it wasn't bad enough that she had caught him in bed with some skank two months before their wedding, this certainly was the icing on the crap cake she'd been served ever since. Why couldn't

20

she just have one thing go right? Would that be too much to ask for?

"Yes, look." He pulled out official looking papers and handed them to her. "It was transferred legally. I didn't know that there was another occupant." The man's lower lip looked apologetic, but the rest of him was clearly showing her he didn't plan to move. Why did she get the feeling he was not being completely honest?

Taking a closer look at the papers, she realized he was telling the truth. The paperwork even showed that it had been legally transferred. Crap! Had she missed that in her reservation? Caydence took her papers out, but she did not see anyone's name other than hers and Dalton's. The dates on the papers were only a few days off, which meant Dalton had received his confirmation and switched them on his end.

"Unbelievable! That asshat!"

"Whoa, relax. I'm sure we can find some kind of resolution." He looked as if he truly did not mean to upset her. "I'm sorry about the confusion."

"I'm not leaving. This is my vacation. I paid for it a long time ago. I paid for his ticket too." That was the one thing that Dalton had let her pay for. He had taken care of the wedding. She had booked the cruise and paid with it from the *measly* pay she received from her work. His words, of course. How dare he sell something he didn't even pay for?! "Ugh!"

"Calm down, honey." The man held up a hand, as if he were afraid she was about to come unhinged.

"Don't call me honey! Well, you'll just have to find another room." Right? That could be arranged. No problem. Remove him from her room and go about her way. There was still time to resolve this. She heard the toot of the ship's horn, and felt a slight shift of movement under her feet. "We're moving!"

"We've been moving for quite some time now."

Caydence felt like the room was spinning around her. There had to be a resolution. This could not be the way her vacation started. It was a metaphor for her life right now. Just when she thought she was making some headway, everything always reverted back to the beginning. Caydence was near shaking. "You need to find another room."

"Are you kidding me? Didn't you hear? This cruise is overbooked. There's no way I'm giving up my spot. Plus, as you can tell, the ship has already left port."

Crap. Caydence closed her eyes and tried to let the steam from her head cool, before she looked like some cartoon cat with smoke coming out her ears. "I'm sorry. I know it's not your fault."

She felt a tear pool at the corner of her eye and willed an arctic wind to come swooping in and freeze it before it fell on her face. Even here, Dalton had obliterated her calm. She had taken one step forward and ten steps back in the blink of an eye. Gripping her nails into her palms, Caydence tried to retain control over herself. She refused to let Dalton win this too.

"Maybe we can make this work?" He truly looked sorry this time.

Maybe she should let the tear fall and see how sorry he would be. It was doubtful that would have any effect, though. Caydence no longer expected any man to have a heart. Not to generalize, but from her close personal experience, they tended to rip her heart out, throw it on the ground, and stomp on it until it was barely beating any more. She took a deep breath and tried to calm herself.

"What do you suggest?" Caydence looked at him speculatively, wondering if something sensible would come out of his mouth, and the more she thought about that mouth, the more she wondered if it was a soft as it looked.

"Well, we could see if they have a cot that we could put in here. Take turns sharing the bed?" He gestured to the bed, and even though his words were unassuming, the glint to his eyes told her he wasn't as innocent as his words relayed.

"Sharing the bed?" Caydence's imagination took over as she imagined sharing that very same bed with the sexy man sitting on the edge of it. She may be annoyed beyond belief, but she wasn't blind.

His face was chiseled and strong, his black hair long enough to run her hands through the top and to yank backwards with the longer strands at the back. And what was up with those lashes? They made his amber eyes look almost enchanting. She felt a flush rise to her face, and was brutally reminded that it had been quite some time since she had slept with any man. He certainly fit the bill of a walking fantasy, if that was something she was actually looking for, but Caydence had sworn off men for now. They were more trouble than they were worth.

"I didn't mean that we should actually share the bed at the same time." But his eyes spoke differently.

Right. Now he was lying. She saw the way his eyes had

lit up when she repeated the question. This man, whoever he was, would have no qualms having a fling during a cruise. Maybe it was the whole reason he'd purchased the ticket from Dalton. She still had no idea how his secretary had gotten ahold of the ticket. No matter. The joke was on him, though. As Marianne had said earlier, this was a couple's cruise. Fat chance he would find any other single woman on board.

Seeing as how Caydence had used her vacation to go on this cruise, something she had wanted to do most of her life, the twenty-eight-year-old was not ready to turn tail and run away from this challenge. No. Not Caydence. She'd face it head on and do what she could to still have the time of her life, foiled honeymoon or not, damn it. "I'm sorry, what was your name again?"

"Tyler."

"Well. I'd say it was a pleasure meeting you, but our circumstances…." It would have been a pleasure to meet him under different circumstances. These were ridiculous ones, though, if she were actually looking to lose herself in the depths of those golden eyes.

"Right. And you are?"

Did his teeth have to be so perfectly white? Planes could be taken down with one glint from the sun sparkling on those things. Right now, she was having trouble thinking about what he had just asked her. Was it her name? "Caydence."

"That's a unique name." Tyler smiled at her just a little less, allowing her reason enough to take a deep breath.

"Thank you, I think. So…which closet are you taking?"

"So you're going to stay?" He actually looked pleased

with the idea.

"This is the first vacation I've had in five years." She had made up her mind. The show must go on, or something like that. If she were lucky, she'd spend very little time inside this cabin, and more out on the decks above.

"Same. I've been too busy working."

"I was waiting on the wrong thing, apparently." Caydence didn't feel the need to tell him what had happened to her. He didn't need to know her circumstances. Hell, she didn't even want to remember them.

"Ah, nasty break-up?"

"What do you think? We're in one of the honeymoon suites...." Caydence continued to the doors that opened onto a small veranda balcony. Even in her annoyed state, she found the view breathtaking. "It's beautiful."

"Yes, it is." His voice was so quiet that Caydence turned around to see him staring at her.

"If you promise not to maul me, I think we could share the bed. It's large enough." She wasn't sure why she blurted that out. She almost regretted it the moment she did. It wasn't like he was one of her girlfriends that she could curl up next to without any worries. But there was some malfunction in her brain at the moment. *Handsome stranger, no strings,* whispered in her head, and she tried to shake that thought out as soon as it came. That wasn't a thought that belonged in her head. She was much too rational for that.

When he breathed a visible sigh of relief, Caydence felt like laughing. Clearly he didn't like the idea of sleeping on the floor or a cot any more than she did. At another time, maybe another world entirely, she would have been more than happy to spend her time with someone as devilishly handsome as Tyler. Although more than likely she would be much too boring for his tastes. He did have a slight air of adventure to him.

"So, truce?"

"Truce." She turned around and walked over to the closest closet and found his clothes hanging inside. "Was I really that late?"

"No, I just got here really early," he teased her.

"I'll just take the other one then."

Caydence started to unpack her things, aware that Tyler was watching her every move. She found this a little unnerving. Suddenly, she felt underdressed. Or overdressed, depending on how his eyes were actually examining her. This thought disturbed and thrilled her at the same time. When was the last time she had actually felt attractive to the male species? There was a fine difference between being shown off as arm candy and actually being treated as something desirable.

With all these thoughts swarming through her head, Caydence was resigned to the fact that this would in fact be the longest cruise ever. But what else could she do except turn lemons to lemonade? The idea of making lemonade with him flashed in her head, and suddenly her mind was going places it should never be allowed. Rubbing lemons in places they should never be...it was safe to say it had been a really long time since Caydence had been with a man if she was having a sexual fantasy with lemons. Caydence jumped when Tyler cleared his voice.

"Do you want to get a bite?"

"A what?" She blinked as his words caught through her fog. What was it he had said? And was that button undone a few minutes ago?

"Some food." His grin didn't seem to meet his eyes. Was he having the same problem? Probably not. He looked like a man who got laid a few times a week. Lucky.

"Oh, right. You don't have to entertain me. I'm not your problem to deal with." She closed the closet door and turned to face him.

"We both need to eat. And between you and me, I'd rather not go alone. Too many happy couples everywhere."

He had a point. The whole ship was bound to be filled with love crazed couples. She would have been one of them. She closed her eyes and tried to remind herself not to go there. Instead, she turned her thoughts to the man standing in front of her. Her curiosity got the best of her. "No girlfriend?"

"Married to my work." He grinned and held up his hands in defense.

How in the world could a man that sexy spend all his time at work? Surely there were a few women lining up at his door. Caydence called bullshit on that, because she knew if given enough encouragement she just might break her resolve of swearing off all men. She gave in for the moment. What harm would there be in just getting some food? "Okay. Food does sound good, and I've paid for the full gamut. Might as well enjoy it."

"That's the spirit." He slid his card into his pocket.

Caydence watched him walk to the door, and suddenly

felt guilty when he turned to find her checking out the way his tight jeans fit his bottom. She cleared her throat. "Lead the way."

He gave her a knowing smile. "This way, my dear."

"*My dear*?" Her eyes narrowed on him.

"Just in case they assume we're a couple," he suggested.

Actually, that wasn't a bad idea. Caydence followed after him and fought the urge to slap him on the ass. She felt a rosy heat fill her cheeks. "Okay, *honey*."

Chapter 4

As they made their way up to the closest buffet, Caydence saw a lot of couples standing all around gathering their food. She wondered if she could just take a plate back to her room, but seeing as how no one else seemed to be doing that, she knew she would just have to suck it up. Caydence continued to follow Tyler's lead, seeing as how he looked quite at home here.

They gathered their food in silence, their eyes barely meeting. Caydence carried her plate through the crowd of people and sat down at a table next to him. Looking down at her plate, she realized she had barely put anything on it.

"Not hungry?" he asked her quizzically.

"I haven't been eating much lately," she offered softly.

It was true. Her stomach had been in perpetual knots since the day she had walked in on Dalton, filled with doubts and insecurities she could not seem to push away, even with the anger that spiraled inside her. One day Caydence was going to completely self-destruct if she wasn't careful. Sometimes she felt it winding up inside her, like a crazy coil ready to spring. So far she had managed to keep all her major freak outs in the privacy of her own home, or with her friend Janelle, who seemed to encourage them.

"You should eat more. You'll waste away if you're not careful."

What did he know about it? And it wasn't like she was tiny to begin with. Caydence was a curvy girl, just barely over the top of where her BMI should be—not that she ever put any stock in that. The point was, Caydence was clearly not fading away. She bit off a snarky comment and decided to go a different route. The poor guy was only trying to be nice, after all. "Thank you for your concern."

Tyler looked a little disappointed with her response, as if he were intentionally goading her. He held up one of the shrimp from his plate. "Here, try this."

Caydence glared at him. "I'm fine."

"I'll keep holding it here until you try it," he warned.

She tilted her head at him. "What if I'm allergic to seafood?"

"Are you?" he asked her.

"No."

"Then what are you afraid of?"

"I'm not afraid of anything."

But she was, and the minute her mouth slid over the shrimp and brushed against his fingers, Caydence felt the fear racing through her body. It was brief, but the contact reminded her that a handsome man was sitting across from her, which in turn brought home the point that she had not had sex with *any* man in quite some time. Her lips so close to

30

his flesh made her feel like a million ants were crawling over her skin, as it came alive with the slight fantasy that started to form in her mind. Why had she even suggested they sleep in the same bed? That was definitely a mistake.

"See, that wasn't so bad, was it?" His eyes were darker than just a few seconds ago, the amber filled with a fire that made him devilish.

"No," she answered truthfully. It wasn't so horrible. She deflected her eyes to her plate and continued to put all her attention on it. Thankfully, Tyler didn't offer her any more food.

When another young couple approached the table, the man addressed them. "Are these seats taken?"

"No, not at all," Caydence answered for them. Having a few more people at the table would be a good buffer. If she focused on them, then she would be able to ignore the man sitting next to her. At least, that was what she tried to tell herself. So far, she was only partially acceptable. He probably wasn't having a problem at all. Workaholics were often oblivious to the outside world. She remembered trying to get Dalton's attention when he was working overtime one weekend. Caydence had even stripped down in front of his computer, hoping to catch his attention, and even when he saw her as naked as the day she was born, he turned back to his work. Now that she thought about it, he probably had already had sex with his secretary or some other mystery woman the entire week before he came to visit her. Asshole.

"I'm Alice. This is George," the woman introduced herself.

Caydence forced herself to focus. The couple seemed to

31

be so comfortable with each other, and so happy it was almost irritating. That should have been her right now, but several things were keeping that from being possible. Sometimes she felt like the universe had pinned a target on her chest, marking her for disaster. Like going on a honeymoon cruise to get away from her misery, only to find she wouldn't even get the solace of her own company.

"Nice to meet you," Tyler greeted them with a smile. He seemed to not notice any of the discomfort his cabin mate was having at the moment.

"Isn't this to die for?" Alice was clearly in awe of her surroundings.

"Alice and I are celebrating our five year anniversary. We've never been on a cruise before."

"How about you two?" Alice asked them exuberantly.

Caydence wanted to jump ship right there. Why had she asked them to sit down? "We're—"

"On our honeymoon," Tyler answered for them. His hand took hers and he brought it to his lips.

"Aww, that's so sweet."

Sweet? Caydence didn't think so. Every inch of her flesh felt like she was on fire, and she knew it wasn't the heat of the sun beating down on her. She tried to pull her hand away, but he refused to let it go. Clearly he was enjoying her discomfort. Caydence could play that game too. "Can I have another shrimp?"

"Of course." Tyler released her hand and held up one of his shrimp.

When her mouth latched onto it, she let her tongue lick

off some of the sauce from his fingers. She felt him jerk his hands lightly. "Delicious. Thank you."

"Any time."

When her eyes met his, she was starting to wish she had not done that. She reminded herself that she had to spend two weeks with this man in her cabin. Perhaps teasing him was not the best route to go if she was going to sleep in the same bed with him. Caydence did not really want to give him the wrong idea...or did she? She was not the kind of woman who slept around. No, not at all. She was closer to a barren desert at this point. Her sex life was so non-existent she could see tumbleweeds rolling past her.

"Remember when we were that precious?" Alice asked her husband.

Caydence tried not to choke on her drink—as if in five years their entire relationship had deteriorated. The two looked as if they were married yesterday, the way she should have looked at this exact moment with Dalton by her side. She looked down at her plate and tried to fight the angry tears that were building behind her eyes. Caydence almost jumped when Tyler put his hand in her lap.

"I'm a lucky man." He smiled at her, and her thoughts seemed to evaporate on the spot.

"So am I, and it wasn't that long ago, Alice." Her husband did not like being put on the spot like that.

Caydence put a napkin to her mouth and wiped away any crumbs. "Well, I think I've had enough."

Tyler stood up with her. "Enjoy your food."

"Enjoy your dessert," teased Alice.

Caydence almost sucked in her breath as she walked away. When they were far enough away, she almost turned on him. "Just what was *that* about?"

"You invited them to the table." His eyebrows rose nonchalantly.

"Are you serious right now?" Caydence was ready to spit.

When he pulled her into his arms and brought his lips down to hers, she almost kicked him in the shin, but when the kiss deepened, she had a completely different reflex. A soft sigh broke free from her lips, and she grabbed his shirt with her fingers. When he pulled away, her mind was foggy.

"What was that for?"

"They were watching." He nodded back to the table.

Caydence had no idea why she felt so deflated. She released his shirt and backed away from him. "I see."

"So what are you going to do for the rest of the day?" Tyler asked her.

"I don't know. I might just lay out on our balcony for a bit. I'm kind of tired." She wasn't, not really, but she really needed an excuse to get away from him for just a moment. He was already throwing a wrench in her plans. His nearness, the soft velvety lips, those golden eyes, they were all working against her sanity. The funny thing was, his kiss had almost rewritten every kiss she'd ever had to this point. Part of her was curious to know what else he could erase from her mind. *No, Caydence. Down girl.* She had just promised they could share a bed without any issue. Maybe she really should see if there was another room.

"Suit yourself. I think I'll wander around a bit." Tyler

winked at her and walked away.

Just like that and he was off. Caydence imagined him to be much like a social butterfly. She was sure he could charm any woman on the ship, married or not. Then again, there were plenty of beautiful woman working on the cruise. Maybe she should wish for that. The busier he was, the less she had to see of him and the more privacy she would have. The less likely she would be to act impulsively. She definitely needed to get her imagination in check.

Caydence tried to weave through the crowds that were milling all around at different places. Apparently, this was what a lot of people did when they first got on the ship. While everyone else seemed hell bent on exploring the ship, Caydence was simply trying to make her way back to the room.

When she finally did, she breathed a sigh of relief. She walked over to the mirror in the small bathroom and splashed some water on her face. "You can get through this, Caydence."

Heaven knows she had already been through one of the worst things any woman could endure. While she had asked Dalton to take care of canceling the wedding, he had refused to believe she wouldn't come through. Apparently, her willingness to give in to his every whim up until that point had only made him think he had the upper hand in their relationship. Caydence had to notify Rosalind herself, who told her that Dalton had told her she was just having cold feet. At one point, Caydence had told her if she wanted to continue with the wedding, it would be an epic fail, because there was no way in hell she would be walking down the aisle with him, ever. When Rosalind had sent her the dress, Caydence figured the woman had either gotten the hint or it was Dalton's way of taunting her from afar. Seeing as how she had refused to talk to him, Caydence would never truly know, which suited her just fine. At least she had gotten past the point of wanting to run him over.

Caydence gripped her hands into fists and fought the urge to slam them into something. "You don't get to ruin this too, Dalton."

A new resolve started to grow inside her. This was not the time to keep dwelling on the past. New beginnings — that's what she was all about. She pulled out her phone and texted Janelle. She wrote like her fingers were driving *Fast and Furious*, Bahama breeze version. When she pressed send, she wasn't disappointed. In the next moment, her phone rang.

"Hello?"

"Are you shitting me?" Janelle almost screamed into the phone.

"No."

"That asshat sold his ticket, the ticket you fucking paid for?" Something smashed in the background.

"What was that?" Caydence asked her.

"The cat. Scared the shit out of me too. Sneaky little bastard."

Caydence giggled as she imagined Simon sneaking up on Janelle. "Remind me to bring him some catnip."

"That's not funny. You know that's like crack to him. I'll never get him off the ceiling. Remember last time?"

She did. The cat had managed to climb up to the largest

cabinet. He had sprawled out on his back and his feet had touched the ceiling like he thought he was walking across it. Caydence giggled. "Thank you. I needed that."

"So...this guy...."

"What about him?" Caydence already knew what her friend was going to say.

"Is he attractive?"

"As sin," Caydence admitted.

"Oooh...interesting."

"I am not going to sleep with him," Caydence interjected. "I mean, we are going to sleep in the same bed, so technically I am sleeping with him—uhm, beside him. Damn it, you know what I mean. Would you stop cackling? You sound like a Halloween prop right now."

"Caydence, don't be a prude. Get laid, will you please? And then tell me all the juicy details."

Caydence's breath sucked into her chest audibly. "Janelle!"

"What? You're not married. Sounds like he isn't either. It's like you're in Vegas. You know how that works. What happens in Vegas, stays in Vegas. Live it up a little. Heaven knows when the last time was you actually had an orgasm."

"Okay, now you're just being mean." Caydence felt her insides twist at her friend's brutal honesty.

"No, I'm just trying to get you to live your life for a change. You don't have anyone to take care of anymore. Just yourself. It's about time you do something for you."

"I'll think about it."

"Crap. I have to go. I think Simon opened the garage door

again. That cat is going to be the end of me. Love you, girl!"

"Love you too!"

Caydence hung up the phone and shook her head. Janelle was right about one thing. It was time to do something for herself. What, she wasn't quite sure of yet, but she figured it would resolve itself eventually.

Chapter 5

Slipping into one of her suits, Caydence applied some sunscreen and walked out onto the balcony with a book and a bottle of water. Having the honeymoon suite did have its advantages. The balcony had enough room for two loungers with a small table in between them. She could stand up and look out at the ocean from the railing, or simply lie down and peer up at the skies above. She chose the latter. The best part was that it had enough privacy that she did not have to worry about anyone staring at her while she laid out in her swimsuit.

She stayed out there for a few hours, alternating sides and reapplying her sunscreen. Caydence was enjoying the open breeze. She was half-tempted to just sleep out there tonight, but she knew it would get much colder when the sun went down. There was also the slight fear that if she did fall asleep out there, somehow she would manage to tumble overboard in her sleep. An irrational fear, but a fear nonetheless.

When she felt her stomach start to rumble, Caydence knew it was time for food. She was just leaving the balcony when Tyler entered from the hallway. The way his eyes roamed over her body made her realize she should have put her wrap on. She felt a little uncomfortable in her skin.

"Did you have fun?"

"Not as much as I would have liked."

She couldn't tell what exactly he meant by that, but she refused to rise to the bait. "I was just about to order some room service. Are you hungry?"

"Starving."

Oh, he looked starving, like the Big Bad Wolf about to devour Little Red Riding Hood. Caydence pursed her lips as she walked over to the closet to find one of her small swimsuit covers. She pulled out a simple black one and slid it over her body. "So, what would you like?"

Tyler visibly blinked. "For what?"

"Dinner. Are you okay? Did you get too much sun?" Caydence walked over and put a hand over his forehead, and pulled back when he flinched slightly. She looked down at her hand. "I'm so sorry. It's just a habit."

He smiled at her. "He was a lucky man to have someone like you looking out for him."

"He never needed me." She brushed his words off, stepped away, and picked up a menu. She didn't really want to talk about Dalton with him. "Want to share a pizza?"

"Sounds good to me." His lips curved into a smile. Tyler sat down on the small couch near the television. He pulled his laptop from his bag and opened it up.

"Working?" She grinned knowingly. While she had finished her blogs for the next few weeks, she had promised to catalog her adventures on the ship while she was gone.

That was one of the challenges Janelle have given her — do something she wouldn't normally do. Caydence had a whole list of them, and that wasn't even including the man who was in the room. Janelle had already texted her to put him at the top of her list, right above zip-lining and parasailing. Lord help Janelle when she got ahold of her. Caydence should never have told her.

"Always." He barely glanced up from his laptop.

"I thought you were supposed to get away from work," she challenged him. Not that she cared what he did. He could work the whole time he was here if he wanted, but then he would have paid for a vacation he never took. Caydence was certainly not going to stay holed up in this cabin with him. Unless…. *Stop it, Caydence. None of that. Single and happily so,* she reminded herself. But the devil on her shoulder told her she was still unattached.

"What shall I do then?" His lips turned up to a half-smile, as if he knew the internal debate going on in her head.

"I thought about watching a movie. You could join me if you wanted." Caydence actually hoped he took her up on the offer. No need to sit here and make mindless conversation. It would be far easier to watch something that could distract her from the handsome stranger.

"Sure. It's been awhile since I've watched anything." Tyler closed his laptop and slid it back inside his bag.

"Me too." She offered a half smile. It was true. She had been so busy rearranging her life that watching television had not been one of her priorities. Keeping busy was always the best bet. Then she wouldn't think about how far her life had sunk into a sluggish pit over the past three years.

"Work?" he asked her.

"In a manner of speaking. I'm a blogger." Caydence waited for him to make some kind of offhand comment about her job choice. It never came. Instead, he looked visibly impressed.

"That's not an easy job. A buddy of mine does that for tour destinations. Keeps him pretty busy."

"Really?" Caydence almost breathed a sigh of relief. Not everyone understood what she did or why she had chosen to do it. She had always loved writing, but knew that penning a book might not bring her enough money to support herself. Instead, she'd used her love for words to create a freelance career for herself.

"Yeah. He makes pretty good money traveling around the world and sharing his experiences."

"That sounds amazing. I do lifestyle pieces for different places. How to pieces, product reviews. That kind of thing. I represent companies that sell from different manufacturers. It's not as fascinating as traveling the world, but I do make a good living from it. What about you?"

"Hedge fund manager for several firms. I do all right myself."

"Do they know you're on vacation? Your bosses?" She crossed her arms over her chest and gave him that boy-caught-in-the-cookie-jar stare she might give someone she knew better than him. Why did she feel the need to fuss over him? He was a perfect stranger, after all.

"Yes, I do. I'm the boss." Tyler ran a hand through his hair and gave her a roguish grin. "I guess old habits are hard to break."

"Tell me about it." Three years of bad habits had brought her to this very situation. She picked up the phone to order a pizza. "What do you like?"

"Everything…." His words seemed to imply that he was talking about more than pizza.

Caydence reminded herself that her imagination was running away with her, but just to clarify, she called him out on it. "On the pizza?"

Tyler gave her a rueful smile. "Load it up."

Caydence spoke into the phone. "Yes, thank you. One supreme pizza, hold the onions. Suite 920. Yes, the honeymoon suite. Oh yes…well, thank you."

Caydence hung up the phone and rolled her eyes. Was her entire vacation going to be congratulations on a love that had fizzled out long ago? A constant reminder of what it should have been, instead of what it had become?

"More congratulations?" Tyler asked her knowingly.

"Yes." Her voice was dull and flat.

"His loss."

"What?" Caydence had been slightly distracted when he spoke—trapped inside a million memories that would never let her go, that's the way she felt.

"Nothing. What should we watch?" He started to flick through the television programming. "Action, adventure, comedy, drama?"

"How about an action movie?" Caydence had watched plenty of *Lifetime* movies to last her the rest of her own life. Every one of them had a happily ever after that eluded her.

She sat down on the couch next to him and gave him a soft smile. "This one looks good."

"Sounds good."

If her being near him bothered him, he never showed it. The distance between them was barely adequate, but Caydence did not like the idea of sitting down on the bed right now. It only made her think about the fact that they would share it that night—unless one of them slept on the couch. Caydence looked down at it and realized whoever slept on it would not get much sleep. There was barely enough space for the two of them to sit without brushing close together.

When a knock sounded on the door, Caydence almost jumped out of her skin. Tyler took pity on her and went to retrieve their food. He returned with arms loaded with the pizza and a basket of goodies. His eyes met hers.

"Sorry about this. She said it was supposed to be here before we checked in."

Caydence looked at the basket he set down in front of her. A romantic basket that she had not remembered, filled with a few things that couples might find interesting. Things that only made her feel like blushing. "Is that a…?"

"Pretty sure, yep." He looked away from her.

Box of condoms. Caydence was almost mortified at this point, and could feel a blush rushing over her face. "Oh, dear lord."

"Some nice chocolates in here," he pointed out. "If you like chocolate."

"Maybe later. Pizza first." She did not meet his eyes this time. Heaven forbid he take her words to mean that later something else might happen. "Chocolate, that is."

"Pity," she thought she heard him say.

Did that mean he was interested in something else? Maybe she should sleep on the couch. Caydence took one of the plates and started to load it up. She couldn't remember the last time she'd had pizza, especially one that was piping hot. After she ate a few pieces, she saw Tyler looking at her with a soft smile on his face. "What?"

He leaned in closer to her, so close she thought he might be trying to kiss her. Instead, he used his thumb to wipe the corners of her mouth. "Just a little sauce."

Caydence felt her nerve endings electrify. Had it really been that long since she'd actually been touched by a man? Or was this some mystical spell he was weaving over her? She looked away before she could meet his eyes.

"I won't bite, Caydence."

"Won't you?" her voice answered. She put a hand over her mouth. "I'm sorry. I didn't mean to say that."

Tyler chuckled. "Oh, dear Caydence. You are simply precious."

"Precious?" Her right eyebrow rose speculatively.

"Yes. Precious."

"I think you're mocking me," she accused him softly.

"Not at all." He moved closer to her face again.

Caydence backed away and put her hand up. "Do I have more sauce?"

"No. I'm going to kiss you."

"Oh...." Caydence could have moved away, and probably should have, but she remembered the way his lips had felt

45

hours earlier, and she was curious. What did she have to lose? "Just a kiss?"

"Just a kiss, Caydence," he promised her.

His lips touched hers softly at first, and Caydence could taste the tomato sauce on them, which made her feel like giggling. When he wrapped his hands around her to pull her closer, Caydence thought about pushing away, but it had been a lifetime since she had last felt attractive to a man. She sighed against him as his tongue slipped into her mouth. Not entirely sure how long the kiss lasted, Caydence was nearly breathless when he released her.

"That was…umm…thank you." Her voice came out in an almost inaudible whisper.

"At your service." He looked as if the kiss had shaken him slightly too, but only briefly. Soon, his face was covered in the same boyish charm he usually broadcasted.

Caydence slid back to her side of the couch, the side that was only four inches away from him. She was trying to still the thoughts racing through her mind. Caydence did not usually fantasize about handsome strangers. Then again, none of them had kissed her so thoroughly. No one had, not for years. Caydence was starting to realize she had missed out on quite a bit while waiting for Dalton to finally come to his senses and make her an honest woman. Funny that, a dishonest man trying to make an honest woman of her. The irony was not lost on her.

When she finally was too tired to think, Caydence stretched. It had almost been a battle of wills to see who would make their way to the bed first. Caydence lost. She yawned and tried to stand up. "I think I'm going to sleep now."

"Good night." Tyler looked exhausted too, but he made no move to get up.

Caydence realized he was being a gentleman, and while she felt guilty about that, she was not going to tell him to come to bed any time soon. She quickly dressed into something more comfortable than her swimsuit, then walked over to the bed and pulled the covers up so that she could slide underneath them. The cool sheets were bliss as she snuggled into them. She took one of the extra pillows and put it in the middle of the bed as a divider. In a matter of minutes, she was out like a light.

Chapter 6

When she woke up in the morning, she was surprised to find that Tyler's side of the bed had not been slept in at all. She stretched and yawned. Caydence was surprised at how well she had slept. She had always assumed that she might get seasick on a cruise, but so far she hadn't had a problem. She was thankful, for that was the last thing that she needed to happen right now.

Sitting up in bed, she made a small mental list of all the things she wanted to do today. The ship was filled with things she had never done before. Caydence was resolved to doing as much as she could. When would she have another chance to cross off some of these bucket list items? As she looked over at the couch, she saw that Tyler was sleeping there. She pursed her lips and wondered why he would want to sleep on that stiff thing when there was a comfortable bed right here. Did he not want to be near her? He hadn't given her that impression yesterday. But then again, maybe he was just being polite.

Ah well, so much for the top of the list. She smirked.

Janelle would be disappointed, but Caydence was relieved. She certainly didn't need to throw a holiday fling into her arsenal of grand mistakes. Walking over to the closet, she looked for something to wear that was practical. What should she do today? Zip line? Surfing? Rock climbing?

It was less than likely that she would do all of those in one day. Maybe she should do the zip line and some rock climbing. Looking down at her arms, she smiled weakly. She knew that it would take her half the day to climb any wall. She may be in good shape, but her arms were not that strong. It would certainly make for a funny story.

Looking around the room, she realized that there was no really good place to get changed. She could maybe take her things into the bathroom, but the only thing that was covered was the toilet area, as it was a small water closet set up with the shower existing just outside it. Glancing over at Tyler, she saw that he was still asleep. If she was fast, she could get dressed before he even woke up. That was probably the only choice, because she didn't look forward to changing in a tiny bathroom. With her luck, she would end up tripping and landing head first in the toilet.

First Caydence pulled off the pair of sleep shorts she had slid on last night. She chose a pair of underwear that would not ride up her crack. Constantly digging underwear out was not attractive at all. She leaned over and looked at Tyler, to make sure he was still asleep. He seemed to be breathing just as peacefully as before. Thank goodness.

Pulling her shirt over her head, she undid the clasps of her bra. Why in the world had she gone to sleep in her bra?

49

Having wires poke into her skin all night was not a picnic, not to mention the little red lines from where she rolled over onto them as she slept. She rubbed her skin and flinched slightly. Caydence let the straps slide over her shoulders and felt the cool air touch her breasts. She shivered slightly and rubbed her arms before looking for a replacement. Reaching in to one of the drawers, she pulled out one of the sports bras she had brought with her. Probably the best choice for her today.

She turned around to put it on and saw two golden eyes devouring every inch of her body. When they rose to linger on her chest, Caydence felt her nipples start to grow. She could not break the trance, no matter how hard she tried. Seeing the desire in his eyes was like a fresh of breath air.

Taking a deep breath, she turned away from his glance and pulled the sports bra over her head. She threw a black T-shirt over it and reached for a pair of shorts, fully aware that he was getting a good view of her ass right now too. She was instantly thankful that she had not worn one of the more risqué pairs of underwear. When she turned around, she did not dare look at him. "Sorry, there's not enough room in the bathroom."

"Don't apologize." He sat up.

Her breath nearly caught in her throat. Caydence could see that either he had morning wood or was clearly affected by the sight of her nearly naked body. Not nearly as affected as she was right now, seeing he was half-dressed himself. His naked chest—it was definitely what she considered chiseled in the right proportions, enough to make her want to slide her hands down it. She closed her eyes and tried to shut the image out of her head.

"Everything okay?"

"Hmm?" Her eyes flashed open.

"You seem out of sorts." He had a half smile on his face at her discomfort.

Caydence refused to rise to the bait. She walked over and sat down next to him to put her shoes on. When she leaned over, she knew he could see her breasts from where her neckline plunged. She heard a slight intake of breath and tried not to react to it. When she sat up, she saw the humor was gone. "You slept on the couch...."

Caydence felt like a moron. After that moment, that was probably not the right thing to mention. What was she doing? This was madness, like baiting a crocodile with fresh meat. She knew he was dangerous, and if she ever offered him a bite, he might devour her whole.

"I didn't want to disturb you. You were sleeping so peacefully."

"You wouldn't have...disturbed me." That wasn't true. Even in the morning light she knew that his very presence disrupted her thoughts. She could not afford to let her mind lead her down that path, no matter how much Janelle tried to get her to.

"So, what are your plans for the day?" he asked her.

"Well, first I'm going to get something to eat."

"Then?" Did he sound hopeful?

"I have a few things to check off my bucket list."

"Oh?" His eyebrow rose curiously. "Like what?"

"Well, I promised to blog about some of my adventures

51

here on the ship. Do some things I wouldn't normally do." Well, that certainly didn't sound any better. Caydence felt a blush rise to her face. She couldn't remember ever being so easily embarrassed.

"Like what? Anything I can help with?" His eyes seemed to twinkle, but his voice was innocent enough.

"Zip lines, rock climbing, surfing."

"What about skydiving?" He challenged her.

"Never been. Have you?"

"No, but I read in the pamphlet that they have a simulator here. Maybe you should add that to your list."

"Hmm. That's not a bad idea." She made a mental note to add that to her list.

"Care for some company?" he asked her.

"Why, so you can laugh at me when I fall on my ass?" she teased him.

"I would do no such thing." He held up his hand as if making a solemn pact.

"Liar," she giggled. "I'd forgive you, mostly because I intend to laugh my ass off doing it."

"That's the spirit." His smile was captivating.

"You're something else," Caydence blurted out, then immediately regretted it.

"So are you."

"You sure you're not attached?" Again, what the hell was her mouth thinking? She needed to staple it shut.

"Not at the moment. Nothing weighing me down."

"Ah…I see." So he saw a woman as a weight, something limiting him. Perhaps that was the truth. A man as handsome as he was had probably had more than his fair share of relationships. Did he cheat too? Not like most women wouldn't throw themselves at him.

"What do you see?" He asked her curiously.

"Nothing." Caydence bit her tongue.

"I'm not like your ex, Caydence. I actually want someone in my life. I just haven't found what I'm looking for." He looked thoughtful, as if he were trying to think about what his next words might be.

Before he could speak, she put her hand on his lap. "You'll find her someday. I'm sure of it."

His eyes met hers. "I hope so."

"Well…." Her word came out in a squeak when she thought his mouth was about to lean toward hers. "Time to get moving. Daylight's burning. I've got a list of things to get through. I'm going to go eat some breakfast."

"Chicken."

"What?" She turned to look at him. "Did you just call me a chicken?"

"I did." His eyes were like liquid fire.

"Am not. I'm not afraid of anything." She felt like crossing her arms like a petulant child.

"Then kiss me."

"What?" she squeaked. "You're hilarious. I'm not going to —"

He captured her mouth mid-sentence, his lips soft against her own. She closed her eyes and remembered what Janelle had told her. Risk. It was an important part of life. Taking them wasn't so easy to do, but sometimes the reward was worth it.

This was one of those times. She couldn't remember the last time she was thoroughly kissed so early in the morning.

When she broke away from his kiss, she was having trouble gathering her thoughts. "Why did you do that?"

"A woman with such kissable lips should never be neglected," he told her.

His words took her breath away. She didn't know what to say. She should probably be mad at him for taking liberties with her, but her heart was pounding deliciously for the first time in forever. While she wanted to lean over and delve deeper, her common sense broke in. "I'm not easy."

"I'm willing to put in the work. Somehow I think the reward will be worth it."

Caydence let out a small huff of air. "You're sure of yourself."

"Nothing's ever a sure thing. So, breakfast, and then—?"

"Rock climbing," she finished his sentence. She ignored his chuckle when she stood up. "I'm going to go eat."

"I'll be up in a few minutes. Save me a seat?"

Caydence sighed in defeat. "Okay."

Chapter 7

When he joined her at the table, she gave him a half smile. She was still in her head a little for a couple of reasons. One, he was probably the most devastatingly handsome man she had ever met, and two, she was absolutely terrified of heights. Not that she really wanted to admit that to anyone. Janelle knew — that was why she had challenged her to face her fears. That was sure easier said than done.

"Cat got your tongue?" he asked her.

"Just thinking about what I'm going to write about." That was partially true. She was thinking about that, but she was also thinking about him.

"Hmmm…well, the food is good. The company is nice too." He winked at her.

"I suppose," she teased him.

"You're eating more," he commented.

Caydence suddenly felt a little self-conscious as she moved her fork around her plate. "There's a lot to choose from."

"Tired of the same old thing?"

"Yes," she answered without thinking. She knew it was a double entendre, but she didn't care. Let him think what he wanted—he was likely to anyway. She looked at the brochure in her hand. "Looks like I'll have to sign up for the zip line. Rockwall is first come first served."

"Why don't you go put in for the zip line, and then do the rock wall while you are waiting?" He suggested.

"I like how you think, Tyler."

"You can say that again."

"What?" Caydence blinked.

"My name. I like the way you say it, Caydence."

She nibbled her lip. Had she said it any differently than any other person would have? When she released her lip, she saw he was staring at it. "You make me self-conscious."

"Don't be. I think you're charming."

She glared at him. "Stop it."

"What?"

"Trying to pick me up." That was what he was doing, wasn't it? He probably used that line on a dozen other women, and that was probably lowballing it.

"Is that what you think?" He smirked at her. "Okay, so compliments are off the table. Duly noted."

Did he look a little hurt? She had to be imagining it. "I'm sorry. I didn't mean to upset you."

"No worries." He held his hands up in front of him.

"I'm just not sure what this…," she gestured between the two of them, "is."

"Whatever you want it to be, I suppose." Tyler was being open and honest.

She looked away, suddenly feeling like she was put on the spot. "Look...I should be clear with you. I haven't dated in...hmm.... Close to three years. So I'm rusty for sure, and wouldn't even know what one felt like. I'm pretty sure that is not what this is. We're just two people occupying the same space."

"In a manner of speaking," agreed Tyler.

"Good. Now that that's cleared up, I'm going to sign up for the zip line."

She stood up and walked away, not really inviting him, but not arguing with his presence as he walked next to her. Caydence actually didn't mind his company, as long as he didn't start looking at her with those sinful eyes. Kind of hard to avoid them, as they were like attractive pools in the middle of his gorgeous face. Honestly, he could have been a rock star or a model with the way his hair pushed back from his face and somehow stayed in place, even with the breeze blowing around them. She was envious of those hair products for sure, because none of her hair was staying where it was supposed to. Caydence kept tucking her hair behind her ears absently.

When they made it to the zip line, Caydence looked at the schedule. "Do you have any available times?"

The woman at the counter barely looked at her as her eyes ran up and down Tyler, who was standing next to her. "Hmm.... Actually, we had a last minute cancellation, if you'd like to go now. But we only have one spot. You can go solo or tandem."

"Tandem?" Caydence almost gulped. She wasn't quite sure what was more frightening to her. Finally, her fear of heights took over. She looked up at him with a slight grimace. "Don't imagine you'd want to go too?"

His eyes were teasing her. "And miss the sight of you flying through the air?"

Caydence felt the color leave her face the more she thought about how high up the line was. He must have sensed her fear, for he put a hand on her arm.

"Sign us up." Tyler squeezed her arm.

"Really?" She gave him an appreciative smile. "Thank you."

"Of course — have to help you face those fears. How many things do you have to cross off the list?"

"Almost too many to count, actually." She giggled nervously.

"Okay, you two. If you just walk to where Tim is standing, he'll get you sorted out. Just sign this waiver first."

"Waiver?"

"You know, in case we fall." Tyler chuckled when he saw her pale face. "Don't worry, we're not going to fall."

"We better not." She punched him playfully on the arm.

"Don't worry. I'll catch you," he teased her.

"Who's going to catch you?" She countered.

"Good point. But look, they're doing just fine." He pointed to the tandem couple that was coming back across the line.

"Fine."

"It will be fine," he promised. He reached for her hand and she let him.

They stayed there for a few moments, holding hands as they waited for their turn. She was surprised to find comfort in that single gesture. She couldn't really remember the last time she'd held someone's hand. Her father's hand when she was eight? It was a public display of affection that had always been lost on her. Right now, it occurred to her that it did have a time and place. Even though they weren't a real couple, she felt safe with the one small gesture.

"You're up here," the attendant gestured to the first harness.

Tyler stepped up and let the man attach him in securely. He sat down as he was instructed, and waited for Caydence to be strapped in on top of him. "You coming? Or are you chicken?"

She eyed him warily as she stepped closer to him. Caydence wasn't sure that sitting in his lap was something she really wanted to do. Right now, she was actually more afraid of that than flying through the air. She sat back and relaxed into his lap, and felt his heat behind her. Yes, this was clearly a bad idea, especially considering how well she fit in the curve of his body. She could smell his cologne, and it was intoxicating.

"All right. Just wrap your arms around her and grab on. Keep your legs out straight," the man told them.

"Got it," Tyler answered as he wrapped his arms around her.

She flinched slightly. "Sorry."

"You sure are jumpy," he teased her.

"Am not." As his mouth almost grazed her ear, she jerked again. "Okay, so maybe I am slightly jumpy."

He chuckled. "Relax."

Easy for him to say. Her whole body seemed to be on fire, and she had no one but herself to blame. If she had not brought him along, she wouldn't be teased by his proximity. The only thing that made her feel better was that she could sense he was not as unaffected as she first thought. As they started to zip through the air, she felt a slight bulge under her. She may have wiggled slightly to make his discomfort a little worse, but she would never admit it.

As the wind zoomed past her, Caydence started to feel exhilarated. She started giggling uncontrollably, and Tyler's hands held her tighter to him. Soon she felt his chuckles rumbling against her.

"Whooo!" she cried out as they continued to glide through the air.

When they landed on the other side, she was still laughing. She turned to find him smiling at her. She had the distinct feeling he was going to kiss her, but she turned away before he could. Did he just whisper chicken? What was she going to do with him?

As the buckles came undone, Caydence leapt from his lap and turned around to meet his knowing eyes. Okay, so she was a little skittish around him, but that wasn't her fault, not really. He made her uncomfortable and comfortable at the same time. He was a mystery that she wasn't sure she wanted to solve.

"So?" he asked her.

"So what?"

"How did it rank?" He asked her with a twinkle in his eyes.

"I wouldn't mind doing that again." It was true. She'd had a blast, probably more so because she had been secure in his arms, not that she would ever admit that aloud.

"Time to climb a wall?" He suggested.

"Yes! Definitely."

She gave him a big smile that she felt from head to toe. Caydence was having more fun than she'd had in a very long time. It was good to feel impulsive. Without thinking, she grabbed his hand and drug him through the crowd of people. When she realized what she'd done, she released it.

"Oh, sorry."

"Don't be." His lips twitched slightly.

Feeling impulse strike, she leaned over and kissed him on the cheek. He seemed taken aback.

"What was that for?"

"For being a good sport." She gave him her brightest smile.

"Any time." He seemed to truly mean it.

Caydence was feeling more carefree than she had in a very long time. By the time they made it back to the room, she was more than ready to climb into bed to get some sleep. She put the pillow in the middle of the bed, just in case he decided to join her. Her eyes drifted closed and she sighed softly before falling into a deep sleep.

As she slept, she dreamt of the handsome stranger with golden eyes that reminded her of a wolf on the prowl. Even in her sleep, Caydence was undressing him with her mind. She saw a flash of his half naked body hovering over her. As the dream continued, he moved his silky lips all over her body.

Her arms held on to any tangible piece of him, as dream Tyler mastered every inch of her body, playing her like a well-tuned violin. In her sleep she tossed and turned, as ghost Tyler ravished every inch of her body.

She woke up as the bed moved slightly. Caydence was gripping the pillow just as she had the dream man just minutes before. She found Tyler sitting on the edge of the bed. "Tyler?"

"I thought you called out...I just wanted to make sure you were all right."

She flushed furiously. "Oh. Sorry. I didn't mean to wake you."

"Nightmare?" His eyes told her that he clearly knew it was no such thing.

She bit her lip, as if that would help settle the throbbing between her legs. Caydence blushed slightly. "Not quite."

"Good, because I would hate to cause a nightmare."

"What do you mean?" Caydence yawned and stretched.

"You called out my name."

"I did no such thing." She refused to meet his eyes.

"My mistake then." He turned away from her and walked back to the couch.

Caydence lay there in mortification. Her dream had been so real, she knew she would constantly wonder what reality was like. Closing her eyes, she half hoped to go right back to her dream. Even if she was too afraid to pursue it in real life, she could still dream about it.

Chapter 8

Caydence took advantage of Tyler's absence to take a quick shower, especially considering it was completely see through. She certainly didn't want to try to take a shower with him there. After last night's dreams, she was still embarrassed. How could she call out his name? All he had done was kiss her. It wasn't like he had done enough to make that wet dream as delicious as it was. She tried not to think about it, or she might start visualizing it all over again. If reality was even half as good as fantasy, she'd probably die from euphoria. Looking down at her breasts, she realized she should probably stop thinking about it.

She was almost done with her shower when the door opened. Caydence shut the water off and quickly grabbed a towel to hide her body from view.

"Sorry, didn't realize...." Tyler turned around and tried to walk sideways to the couch. "Do you need some privacy?"

Caydence snorted. Privacy...this room was not really built to accommodate that. They must assume the only thing people did on their honeymoons was stare at each other. Or

63

spend their time doing what Caydence had dreamt about last night. She almost wondered what that would be like. "I'll just get dressed quickly."

"Let me know when I can turn around."

She could tell he was grinning from where she stood, which implied he had gotten a pretty good look at her. Caydence sighed. Figures. Here she was feeling almost secure with him around, and then she had to go and flash the poor guy.

Caydence dressed as quickly as humanly possible. Today she wore a bikini with one of her sundresses. "Done."

"Decent?" he asked.

"Yep."

"Pity." He turned around to look at her with that flash of a grin she had come to know so well, especially when her ass was dangling in the air on the rock wall yesterday. He was down on the ground staring up at her—ogling was more like it.

"So, ready to get to it?"

His eyebrow rose curiously. "What did you have in mind?"

"Men!" She gritted her teeth and put her hands on her hips. Clearly, anything that could be taken as innuendo was something she should avoid.

"Did anyone tell you you're attractive when you're angry?"

She tilted her head and wrinkled her nose. "Yes—I mean no. Not really."

"I had an idea for this morning."

If he was going to say sex, well…honestly, would she say no? From the email she had gotten from Janelle, she should have already been riding him like a bronco. Thank goodness he hadn't read those emails. She was certainly not going to do that. "What were you thinking?"

"Well, I was thinking laser tag, but now I'm starting to wonder what you thought I was thinking," he teased her.

"Fine. Let's go." Caydence did not respond. She was almost to the door when his arm slowed her down. She turned to look at him.

"I wasn't making fun. I honestly want to know what you're thinking." He put his hand around her back and edged her slightly closer. His lips were close to hers, so close she could feel the heat on her face.

"I refused to answer on the grounds that it might incriminate me," Caydence whispered.

"Really? Was it something like this?" His mouth covered hers and Caydence sighed against him. His hands molded her into him as his tongue sought passage inside her mouth. Their tongues dueled together for what felt like forever, but was only a few minutes.

When her heart was racing dangerously, she put a hand on his chest and pushed away from him. Struggling to gain her breath, she looked up at him with tortured eyes. "Why did you do that?"

"Because you are irresistible." He ran a hand through his hair and let out a sigh. "You ready to go?"

"Where are we going?" She eyed him speculatively. Not that it mattered. As long as it was anywhere but this room, she would be pretty safe.

"I'll tell you when we get there. I promise you can add it to your list."

Caydence followed him reluctantly, her mind racing to all the infinite possibilities still left on the ship. As long as he didn't expect her to karaoke, she would be fine, right? What else could he expect her to do that might embarrass her? Not like she needed much help—she pretty much had a handle on that all by herself.

When he stopped abruptly, Caydence was nearly caught off balance. She looked up and saw a sign. "Laser tag?"

"Unless you're afraid of friendly competition." He winked at her.

"Not at all. You're on." Doing something mindless for a few hours was going to be so much better than what she'd thought about.

The two of them gathered their gear and waited with a small group before they went in. The director was going over safety instructions. This round was boys against girls. Caydence turned around when someone tapped her on the shoulder.

"Oh, hello there," she greeted Alice.

"Ready to take these boys?"

"Definitely." She wrinkled her nose at Tyler. "You're going down."

"If you say so...."

Too late. Sexual innuendo tossed out there. The only one who caught the relevance was Caydence, thank goodness. She refused to let him get to her. She stuck her tongue out at him. "Cheeky."

"Chicken."

Caydence walked around the first wall, looking for the perfect hide out. When she found the perfect corner, she lay in wait. Three men walked by and she took each of them out one at a time. As Tyler walked around the corner, she marked his target.

He held his hand to his chest. "You cut me to the core, woman."

"No mercy for the wicked."

"We'll see about that." He started to move toward her and Caydence shrieked, ducking out of the way before he could get her.

Caydence raced around the corner and slipped out of sight. Let him try to find her, if he could. Hide-n-seek was one of her strengths. She remembered how it had taken hours for her friends to find her when she played. Caydence had mastered the ability to hide in the shadows. The fact that her dress was a dark color worked in her favor, and so did Tyler's white shirt. In the black light he might as well be holding up a big blinking target.

She was doing extremely well, but hadn't seen him in some time. Where was he? Caydence backed up and almost shrieked when she heard his voice right behind her. Her target made a blipping sound, and she grumbled. "Sneak!"

"Damn skippy." He pulled her against him and she sighed.

Turning to face him, she was about to tell him that this was not exactly how the game was played, but anything she would have said was lost the moment his mouth touched hers. In the dark corner, she almost felt like a schoolgirl sneaking behind the bleachers during school hours. As the kiss deepened, she felt his hands on her bottom, pulling her closer to him. When she finally did pull away, her breath was ragged. Every thought she had seemed to float away in the darkness. She heard her target blip and looked up at his wicked grin.

"Oh! Cheater!"

"Hey, all's fair in love and war." He smacked her bottom and took off before she could shoot him back.

"Rat!"

She heard his chuckle as he disappeared in the darkness. By the time the game was over, Caydence had shot him ten more times and taken out any other man she saw in her line of sight. When they stepped out of the game, she gave him the evil eye.

"You're cute when you pout." He winked at her.

"And you'd look cute with my foot up your ass," she grumbled.

"Now, what would you like to do next?"

"Surf," Caydence answered without thinking.

"Really?" He was surprised.

"It *is* on the list." But there were a few other things she had thought about adding to the top. Clearly he was willing, but was she ready to risk it?

"All right then. Let's do it."

She grabbed his hand and pulled him around after her. Caydence felt carefree and adventurous. It was a wonderful feeling. She almost felt reckless. When they got closer, she handed him her phone. "You have to record me, or no one will ever believe me."

"Got it."

As she got on the board, she did just as she was instructed. Laying on the board, she waited for the waves to build. When they did, she stood up on the board and wobbled so much that she fell into the water. She tried a few more times, and by the time she was done, Caydence looked like a drowned rat.

"Did you get it?"

"I did. Also got a text from Janelle asking if you got laid yet." He was clearly teasing her.

"Oh no." Caydence was mortified.

"Don't worry. I sent her a picture and told her I was being a perfect gentleman."

"You didn't."

"I did. What's this symbol stand for?" He held her phone up for her to see.

Caydence saw a wolf followed by a fire. "Uhm, she thinks you're hot."

"I see."

Clearly he was teasing her. "She's a hot mess."

"But you've mentioned me?" He had a goofy grin on his face.

"Oh, dear Lord. Honestly. You're—"

"A pie, apparently."

"Oh my god. I'm going to kill her."

"Speaking of pie. Time to eat?"

"Mind if we just stay in for a bit?" Caydence was starting

to feel like she'd gotten too much sun. "I just want to get out of the heat."

"I can bring something back if you want."

"That would be awesome. Surprise me." She leaned over and kissed him on the cheek.

"What was that for?"

"I don't know," she said absently. "It just seemed right."

"I'll be back to the room as soon as I can."

"Okay. Maybe something cold to drink too? Soda? I'm getting tired of the water."

"Any requests?"

"Anything with some caffeine in it."

"Got it."

It took him longer to get the food than she thought it would. She was halfway through a sappy romance movie when he opened the door to find tears running down her face.

"What's wrong? Did someone die?"

"Yes…her dog died." She pointed to the screen.

"Well that's just tragic. Maybe this will cheer you up."

"Is that Chinese?"

"Sure is." He slid it onto the table. "Maybe we should find a comedy."

"Good idea."

She found it hard to focus on the movie with him sitting so close to her. How many more days could she survive his charm? Would it be so bad to give in to it, if they were both willing? Caydence pushed the thoughts from her head and focused on the movie that was playing before her.

Maybe it was the sun or the full belly, but soon she found

herself drifting to sleep. Caydence awoke to the feeling of being weightless, floating through the air. Her eyelids started to flutter slightly, and she found that she was being carried. She murmured against his warm shoulder. "What...?"

"Shhh. I'm just putting you to bed, Caydence. You fell asleep."

"Mmmmm...," she whispered as her head snuggled into a warm body. The smell of cologne wafted to her nose and she sighed. "You smell good."

She heard a soft chuckle as she was being slowly lowered to the bed. Caydence felt the covers slide over her, and reached out for the body who was leaving her alone. Still half asleep, she whispered, "Don't go."

Caydence felt the bed sink next to her as two arms gathered her close. She sighed as she snuggled against the warm body. Only in a dream state could she admit that she needed another human being close to her. Half asleep, she never knew she had.

Chapter 9

As the morning light started to filter into the cabin, Caydence murmured as she stretched. When her body pushed against something hard and warm, she realized that she was in bed with Tyler's arm wrapped around her stomach. She felt something even harder pushing against her leg as she twisted slightly. Oh dear, was that what she thought it was? She felt his hand grip her closer to him, and turned to see he was deep asleep.

What had happened? Caydence was nearly naked, having only her bikini covering her body. She wiggled slightly and his arms tightened around her. Oh, how long had it been? To have a strong man's arms wrapped around was something she had not even known she had missed out on. Dalton had very rarely held her. Usually, after sex he would just roll away from her and fall asleep. Caydence wiggled her body a little and felt his hands splay across her belly. Her stomach muscles bunched together and released.

Caydence became a little more adventurous than usual. She turned her body slowly and he seemed to accommodate her, as his hands now gripped her back. Gazing up at his face, she saw the shadow of a beard starting to form on his face. Her hand rose to touch it, and she smiled as the scruff started to tickle against the palm of her hands. How could any woman resist such a handsome man? Surely he had quite a few lining up for a chance with him.

Running her fingers along the bottom of his lip, Caydence sighed. Like silk, soft and smooth even in the morning light. She licked her lip and thought about how much she would like to kiss him right now. Was it wrong for her to brush against him? Would he notice? He seemed to be in a deep sleep, probably from overworking himself every day of the week.

Caydence reached up and ran her fingers through his hair. She felt him shuffle slightly under her touch, but his eyes never fluttered. Her hands moved down his face, down to his shoulders that were bunched almost tightly. She fought the urge to massage the tension from them. He carried a lot with him…that she could tell. When she let her fingers run down to the small patch of fur on his chest, she accidentally brushed her fingertip against one of his nipples. The way it perked up should have warned her that she was playing with fire, but Caydence was almost fascinated by the way his body responded to her, even in his sleep.

When he still did not move, Caydence put her lips against his and sighed against them. He was magnificent, even though she would probably never admit it to him while he was awake. She was about to pull away when she realized that his lips were pulling her in deeper. Trapped between an

73

awaking desire and fear, Caydence felt herself being pulled in closer to him. Her breasts were now crushed against his chest.

When she did pull away, Caydence had to work to find her breath. His finger ran over the outline of her swimsuit, and her nipple perked up in response. She wriggled away slightly and put a hand between them. "Stop it."

"What? You were the one molesting me, if you remember," he pointed out with a wry grin.

Caydence let out a gasp in mortification. He was right. "Oh my god, I'm so sorry. I didn't mean to."

"Molest away. It's not every day I wake up to a beautiful woman in my bed."

Caydence put her head in her hands. What was wrong with her? This was not proper at all. She had never nearly mauled a man before. She pushed away from him and sat up on the side of the bed. Tears started to form in her eyes, and she was trying to keep her emotions at bay. "I'm so sorry."

Tyler sat up and kissed the top of her shoulder. "Don't be. I quite enjoyed it."

Caydence could barely hear his words. She was a ball of nerves, wound so tight she would probably break under the right pressure. Caydence should have known this was a mistake when she first walked into the cabin. It had been way too long for her, and he was a temptation dangling right in front of her, in all his aching glory.

"Relax, Caydence." He put his hands on her shoulders and started to massage the tension that was creeping up her spine.

"You shouldn't do that...," she warned him, but she did

not pull away.

"Why not?" His grin could be heard in the amusement in his voice.

"It's been a long time, Tyler. I'm liable to...." She held her hands up in front of her. "Why am I telling you this?"

"Because I'm a good listener?" He suggested. As if sensing a weaker resolve, his mouth trailed a kiss on her neck.

Caydence almost jumped. Oh, how easy it would be to give in to this, but Caydence was not that type of girl. She believed in commitment, happily ever afters. Not that beliefs had brought her any closer to achieving those things. Another tear fell down her face.

Tyler put a hand on her face as he moved to the side of the bed, and kissed the tears away from her face. He pulled her into his embrace and just held her there. "He did a number on you, Caydence."

"It's my fault, really. I should have seen the signs." Her sigh was one of defeat.

Tyler cursed under his breath as he rubbed her back. "He's the fool."

Caydence felt safer in his arms than she ever had in Dalton's. "Wow, you act as if you know him."

He tensed slightly — or was she imagining that? Probably. She imagined a lot of things most days. Like the actual relationship she thought she had been in. That was more imaginary than a unicorn. She'd probably realize that a unicorn was easier to find than a real relationship. Not that she would go looking for one of those any time soon.

She stood up and walk toward the closet. "We should

probably get ready for the day. What should we do?"

"We could stay here all day," he suggested.

She turned to find him giving her a roguish grin. Caydence could not help but chuckle at his attempt. "Stop!"

"Well, we could work on your bucket list. Or you could cross the top one off the list." He winked at her.

She nibbled on her lip as she remembered Janelle's list. "Hmmm...."

"Yes, but you might need a little practice. You seem a bit rusty." Tyler stood up and walked over to her, like a panther stalking its prey.

Caydence backed up slightly and put a hand up as if she was going to stop him. When she ran into the wall of the cabin, she realized she was out of places to run. "What are you doing?"

"I'm going to kiss you, Caydence. Be a good girl, and open up for me."

She barely had time to think before his mouth slid over hers. He spent the next few minutes convincing her with his mouth. By the time he was done, Caydence knew she had no will to resist him, even if she could pretend she did. Would it be so bad to give in to her desire for this handsome man? Probably. With her luck it would snowball out of control. But oh, the fun she would have along the way.

When his lips left hers, Caydence sighed. "You're very good at that."

He grinned at her. "So are you. Would you like some more practice?"

Her heart beat in her chest and she pulled his mouth

down to hers. Was that a groan she heard right before his lips met hers? Caydence let her hands move up to his hair, where they nestled inside his longer locks. She felt her body responding in ways that had been dormant for far too long. Caydence ached for more, but she did not know if she could handle it. He removed the decision from her as he stepped away from her.

"I think I'm going to take a shower."

"Oh."

"Care to join me?" he teased her.

"No thanks." She held her hands up, not because the idea disgusted her, but because she was too close to giving in to keep sane if she was near his naked body.

He chuckled. "Another time then."

Oh God, she hoped so. Her eyes followed him when he headed to the bathroom, and then she blushed when she realized that the shower stall was completely visible from here. Caydence saw him drop his pants, and when he turned to face her, his eyes met hers. Caydence blushed furiously, and turned away from him before he could see the red that was now staining her face.

She heard his chuckle and shook her head. Rogue, from top to bottom. He knew it too. It wasn't like she could hide her desire. She was not that naïve. He knew she wanted him. She was the only one trying to fight against that. If she wasn't careful he would win her over. And then she would…what? Be satisfied? People had flings all the time. Did that make them bad people? Not if they were single and unattached.

That was the problem though. How did she know he

was truly unattached? She didn't. Honestly, she had trouble believing he had no one to warm his sheets. Caydence snuck another glance at the shower, and while she knew she should feel guilty, she could not help admiring his torso. He worked all the time, but that did not stop him from getting to the gym apparently. Her eyes traveled the length of him. All soaped up and wet, watching him was just an appetizer to a delicious meal he had offered up to her with no strings attached.

"Get it together, Caydence," she told herself as she pulled clothes out. This was the second time that she realized that there was no real place to change that would give her privacy. She stepped into the closet and did her best to get changed without any of her body parts showing. Caydence almost fell over twice. The third time was when Tyler snuck up on her.

"Need some help?" He teased her.

Caydence put a hand to her chest and tried to breathe. "You scared me."

She had really thought he would take much longer with his shower. Had she been watching him that long? Or did he take his showers at warp speed? Pity. She could see herself spending a lot more time in the shower with him. Although, here there was a limited supply of water, maybe. Not like a hotel that had water running straight from the ground.

"Sorry," he offered apologetically. He tightened the towel around his waist as he searched through the other closet next to hers.

Caydence saw a drop of water slide down his chest, and she fought the urge to lick it off. What was wrong with her? She was acting like a horny teenager. Of course, if she were she would be getting action. She vaguely remembered those years. The sex had been all right then, only vaguely improved by Dalton. He seemed to have very few tricks up his sleeve. Tyler...she imagined he probably had an entire arsenal.

Tyler pointed to her bra. "You mismatched a few. Want some help?"

"Like hell," she answered as she quickly fixed the back of her bra. This time she made sure they were connected correctly. Then she threw her shirt over her head. Now that she was dressed, she felt a little less exposed. She gazed at Tyler, who was about ready to drop his towel to get dressed. She turned away to give him privacy.

"You can watch if you want," he teased her.

"Oooh!" She grunted as she gathered her fists at her sides.

"Relax, I'm already done," he said near her ear. "Next time?"

She shivered as the heat of his breath touched her lobe. "You incorrigible!"

"Encourage me all you want, Caydence. I'm all yours."

She spun around to face him. "That's not what that word—"

He pulled her lips to his and swallowed the rest of her words. When he had kissed her senseless, he released her. "Po-tay-to, po-tah-to."

Caydence felt her head throbbing as desire raced through her, but she kept it at bay. This was not the time or place. Not yet. She would be a fool if she told herself she would not end up sleeping with him. Every inch of her wanted to, but she didn't want to seem so needy. He could probably smell her lack of experience. She had a virgin reek, even though she had not been one in quite some time. A long time ago, she had been a risk taker. That was before life had taken over. Her need to be successful and provide for herself had overrun her need to actually be happy. Caydence was going to have to alter her aspirations just a little bit. Maybe she could have more than she allowed herself.

"Breakfast?" she asked him.

"Lead the way, fair maiden." When the door closed behind her, he reached for her hand. Caydence looked up at him as if to object, but he brought it to his lips. "Remember, Mrs. Jensen. We're on our honeymoon. You could at least hold my hand."

She giggled at the pretense they had been keeping up while they roamed the ship. "Fine. Mr. Jensen, but don't get handsy."

"Hey, you were the one copping a feel earlier."

Caydence blushed furiously. He was right. She was the guilty party. Not only had she practically molested him, she had spied on him while he was taking a shower. She was a bad girl, but not nearly as bad as she'd like to be if she ever got over the road blocks in her mind. Relaxing her hand in his, she decided it wasn't so bad to pretend just a little bit.

Chapter 10

As they walked to one of the main decks, Caydence could smell the bacon wafting across the air. "That smells good."

"Bacon?"

"Yes! Lots of it."

"I would have taken you for a bagel girl," he teased her.

"Hey, you're the one who told me I needed to make sure I eat," she countered.

"Let your nose lead the way then."

Caydence tried to pull her hand away, but he kept it trapped in his. She felt one of his fingers lightly stroke her palm, and her hand twitched lightly. She had forgotten how ticklish her skin could be. As they walked into the buffet, she finally managed to get her hand free. She didn't miss the slight smirk on his face. What she would give for something to throw at him right now. Maybe a biscuit? Then again, if she started a food fight they might ban her from the buffet.

She loaded up her plate and found a table that was fairly empty. Caydence was not surprised to find him following right behind her. Pretending to be a happy couple, she reminded herself. What did a happy couple do? Besides being ushered around on Dalton's arm, Caydence couldn't remember the last time he had done anything for her really.

"Napkins?" Tyler offered her.

"Thanks." She realized that she had forgotten to pick up some. Had he noticed that, or had he just thought ahead? Either way, it earned him a genuine smile.

"For what?" Tyler asked her.

"You're very thoughtful."

"I am?" He looked genuinely taken aback.

"Yes. You are. Afraid of a compliment?" She asked him.

"Not at all. Just not something I usually get complimented on. Most times it's after…." He looked away with a devilish smile. "Never mind."

Sex. He got complimented on sex. Why did that not surprise her? For such a workaholic, he did have the slight air of a playboy, the kind of man who had enough experience with women to actually make her feel like a virgin. Caydence swallowed some of her orange juice and refused to look at him.

"You blush an awful lot," he teased her.

Caydence was mortified. "Must be the sun."

"Likely story."

"You're having too much fun with this."

"And you are a little wound up," he replied.

Caydence ignored him and continued to eat her food. She was wound up, and it was mostly her fault. Had she not curled up against him overnight, she would not have woken up against him. It would be easy to convince herself that she belonged in the curve of his arms.

"So, what do you want to do today, dear wife?" Tyler asked her, changing the subject.

The fact that he called her wife made her feel a little foolish, for she liked the way it sounded on his lips. She tried not to think about the fact that she should have been Mrs. Something or other by now. "Well, *husband*, I thought maybe we could check out some of the indoor activities, since I seem to be slightly red from the sun."

"Movie?" he suggested.

Caydence felt even more heat fill her face. "No thank you."

"But I like when you fall asleep in my arms." His voice was soft and serious as he reached for her hand. He pulled it up to his face and turned it over to kiss her palm.

Caydence felt a tremor in a place that had been slightly dormant. She crossed her legs uncomfortably. The nerve endings in her hand jumped, and she tried to pull her hand away. Clearly he had noticed how sensitive her hand was when he had stroked it earlier. She closed her eyes and tried to cool the emotions swirling through her. When he released her hand, her eyes flew open.

"Are you finished with your food?"

Caydence blinked. "What?"

"Food. Are you done?" His grin told her that he knew his effect over her.

"Yes." Her answer came out in a soft whisper, and she couldn't quite tell if she was telling him yes take the food, or yes take me now. At this point, her beating heart told her, either answer would have been a true representation of how she was feeling.

"Allow me." He pushed away from his chair and took her plate with his own to return it to one of the bins where the dirty dishes were placed. When he returned he acted as if it were the most normal thing in the world. He held his hand out to her and waited for her to rise. "So, no movie. Pity."

Caydence rolled her eyes. The mood was already broken, thankfully. "Let's explore."

"Sounds good to me."

Caydence let herself be led around a few different decks as they checked out different things for them to do, and while she had asked for indoor activities, she found herself playing giant checkers with him, followed by shuffleboard. She could not remember the last time she had such a carefree time.

"Miniature golf?" He asked her.

"They have that here?"

"Apparently. Another thing for the list?"

"Okay, but I'm not very good." She held up a hand almost defensively.

"I doubt that. You just need the right teacher." His eyes flashed slightly as his dark lashes made his eyes look like melted honey. There was no missing the message there.

Caydence smirked at him. "And you're good at *golf*?"

"Among other things. Care to make a wager?" He asked her as he led her to where the small course was laid out.

"Wager?"

"Winner gets to pick a reward."

"What kind of reward?" Caydence was definitely feeling

wary now.

"Up to the winner, I suppose."

"It can't be anything—"

"That you don't want to do, agreed." He held up his hand to shake on it.

Caydence reluctantly took it, half afraid he would start to kiss her hand again. While he only shook it, she did feel a slight caress of his thumb at her wrist. When he released it, she reached for her own club, rather than wait for him to do it for her. As much as she liked that he was a gentleman, she still felt the need to remind him she was an independent woman.

They played hole after hole, and Caydence was doing fairly well until she could not get the right angle to hole eight. Tyler had managed to get a hole in one. She shook her head at him in disbelief. "How did you do that?"

"It's all about the angle. Here, let me show you." He moved behind her.

Caydence could not fight the urge to sink into his embrace as his arms reached around her to help her with her club. When she bumped into his growing erection, Caydence gasped and tried to wriggle away, but ended up brushing against him further. The intake of breath near her neck made her feel slightly powerful. When his hot breath fanned against her neck, she felt her insides clench. His lips touched down against her skin and Caydence nearly fell over.

"Uhm, okay. I think I got it now. Thank you."

"You're welcome," he whispered softly into her ear with the same hot air that she had felt seconds before.

85

"Incorrigible," she muttered as he stepped away.

"Not much encouragement needed, really. Ready. Definitely willing," he threw out there just as she went to hit the ball. The club hit the ball almost too forcefully, and the ball jumped the little wooden barrier.

"Tyler!" she chided him.

He chuckled. "Hey, I had to catch up on points. I already know what I want."

Her eyebrow rose accusingly. "It can't be *that*."

"My, my. Someone's got their mind in the gutter."

Caydence sighed and retrieved her ball. As she bent down, she noticed he was checking out her behind. Taking her time to pick it up, Caydence smirked at him when she looked up. As she continued to fight fiercely for the lead, she lost at the very last hole and was suddenly wishing she had not taken him up on his offer. "So?"

"What?"

"What did you want?" Caydence asked him.

"A kiss."

"A kiss?" Is that all? Caydence stepped closer, but he held up his hand.

"Not yet. I'll ask for it later."

"Later?" Part of her felt disappointed. She was actually warming up to the idea of kissing him again, even if it meant doing so in front of all these people.

"Yes, as in some undisclosed time or place," he answered her with a rueful smile. "You look disappointed."

She was. "You're enjoying this."

"Absolutely, but since you are so discouraged...." He put

a hand to her cheek and stroked it with his thumb.

When he brought his mouth to her cheek and gave her a little peck, Caydence was ready to smack him. She was about to give him a piece of her mind when his mouth moved over and took the very words out of her mouth. Her entire day had been filled with moments like this, and she started to feel like they were more than the pretend couple he had suggested. Caydence knew that was ridiculous. There was no potential relationship here, but an attraction that was pulling them together like a pair of magnets.

No matter how hard she tried, Caydence knew she could not resist it — not that she believed he would push something on her she didn't want. No, this was partially her fault. One, for not cancelling Dalton's reservation, and two for not looking for another alternative. She was the one who had been inappropriate that morning. If she had not been so sexually starved, this might not have happened. But now that she was here, Caydence realized the path ahead of her did not have to be one filled with dread. Maybe she could actually enjoy herself for a change.

When Tyler broke the kiss, Caydence refused to open her eyes. She did not want to see that playboy smile that was amused at how easily she fell into his arms. She was already berating herself about it.

"Look at me," he whispered.

Her eyelids flew open and she saw the kiss had affected him just as much. There was no amusement anywhere on his face.

"I've wanted to do that all day."

"What?"

"Make you smile."

Caydence brought a hand to her mouth. Was she smiling? A lazy one maybe, for she couldn't remember the last time she had been thoroughly kissed. Sure, Dalton had kissed her before, but not like this. And Dalton — that man did not have enough sizzle to make her feel loopy after kissing him. "Oh."

"So, now what, dear wife?" he asked her.

Caydence had no idea. There were so many activities left, but the only one she really wanted to do, she was too shy to ask for. How easy it would be to give in to the basic desires that were swarming through her. To run her hands through his hair, to nibble on that delectable flesh. The idea of his naked skin touching hers. Caydence wanted so many things that she was too afraid to voice. "Uhm…."

Tyler pulled her close to him and whispered in her ear. "If you keep looking at me like that, I'm liable to throw you over my shoulder and carry you back to the room."

Caydence gasped and shivered slightly. She lay her head on his shoulder and tried to control her breathing. Oh, how she wanted to ask for it, but she was too shy to voice it. Throwing caution to the wind, she let her emotions take the lead.

"Would it be wrong if I wanted you to?"

She heard the intake of his breath. Before she knew it, he was pulling her through the crowd of people.

"What are you doing, Tyler?"

"Taking you back to our room," he answered as they stepped into the elevator. "Before you change your mind."

Caydence was surprised to find they were alone on the

elevator. Tyler took advantage of that as he moved her closer to the wall. His hands touched her face and pulled her into a kiss that was filled with more fire than any of the ones she had experienced with him earlier. She had no idea that was possible. Her leg popped up in reflex and he slid it around him. Caydence put her hand up on his chest and pressed into the hard muscle beneath.

He broke the kiss when the elevator dinged, and pulled away from her. Caydence did her best to reel in the emotions ripping through her. As an older couple walked in, she barely met their eyes. The fact that he brought out a wildness in her was clear. Caydence was almost afraid to see what would happen when they returned to the room.

Her insides were already aching for the promise of what came next. All she had to do was keep her thoughts from turning to where they always did. Consequences. Actions. Words she wanted to stuff so far down inside her that they never saw the light of day. Was it really so bad to take a chance and live just a little more than existing? The walk to the room seemed to take an eternity.

Chapter 11

When they finally made it into their room, Caydence was starting to have second thoughts. It had nothing to do with Tyler, and everything to do with the fact that she was starting to feel a little inexperienced. She could honestly say that she had never been this attracted to any other man. The way he made her heart race scared the hell out of her. What came next, she wasn't entirely sure.

As the door closed behind them, she heard Tyler lock the door. She shivered slightly when his hands touched her shoulders and started to massage the tension that had started to grow.

"Relax, Caydence," his mouth whispered near her ear, and she trembled.

"Wait." Caydence heard his intake of breath and turned around to look at him. All kinds of doubts started to rise up in her head. What if she wasn't as good at this as he was? The way he made her feel was almost dangerous. He clearly had way more experience with this than she did. How would she ever be able to make him feel the way he made her feel? "You should know —"

"You're not going to tell me you're a virgin, are you?" His eyebrow rose curiously, as if the thought might actually excite him.

"No...." Her voice almost came out in a squeak. "But it's been a while. A long while."

"It's like riding a bike, Caydence." His smile faded from his face as he realized she was insecure.

"Yes, but you're like a ten-speed." She gestured to him. "And I'm used to training wheels."

He chuckled at her description. "I assure you, we all work the same way."

Caydence seriously doubted it, but that was beside the point. She looked down at the ground and started to feel foolish. Maybe she shouldn't have said anything. How could she make him understand what she was trying to say? "I just don't want to...."

"What, Caydence? You have to say it, so I know what you mean." Tyler's voice was starting to lose a little patience.

"Disappoint you." She felt more exposed than if she had actually been naked in front of him. Caydence was afraid to get hurt.

He brought his hand to her chin and made her eyes meet his. "Nor I, you."

How in the world could he possibly disappoint her? He was more man than most, but there it was written in his eyes. Caydence didn't understand what was happening. It was like there was part of the conversation she was missing. She didn't want to try to figure out the message hidden beneath. Instead, she did something she would never dream of. She lifted the hem of her shirt and started to pull it over her head. It fell carelessly to the floor, and when he tried to pull her closer to him, she put her finger on his chest and held him at bay. She had to find some way to control the narrative.

"What are you doing, Caydence?" Tyler asked her, his voice sucked in when she removed her shorts.

"I have a confession to make." She remembered the spectacle she had seen this morning—Tyler naked in all his perfect glory. Her heart beat faster just thinking about it.

"Yes?" Tyler asked her, his eyes drawn to the way she bit her bottom lip and nibbled it sensuously.

"I might have caught a peek at you when you were showering."

He chuckled at her words. "I have a confession too."

"What?" she whispered.

"I wanted you to."

Her face flushed and she looked away from him. He forced her to look back up at him.

"There's that blush I love so much. I wonder if I can make you blush from head to toe."

With enough distance between them, Caydence removed her bottoms, then started to work her hands on the back. His fingers stopped her.

"Allow me?" Tyler's voice sounded slightly raw as he pushed her fingers away.

When his fingers skimmed over her back, Caydence sucked in her breath. There was no way he could possibly let her down right here and now. She was almost ready to melt into a puddle at his feet, and he had barely gotten started. As he moved the straps down her shoulders, she felt small kisses following after them, and she felt her toes curl into the floor. As the bra fell to the floor, she stepped back and let him take her in from head to toe. "Do you like what you see?"

Tyler ran his hand through his hair. "Perfection."

Caydence had never heard a man call her perfect before. She liked the sound of it. Stepping closer to him, she rested her head against his shoulder. She smelled his cologne and sighed. When she lifted her head, his mouth covered hers in a gentle kiss. His hands moved down her back in a gentle caress, and she felt them graze her behind. When they gripped each cheek and pulled her closer, he deepened the kiss. Though she was the only one without clothes, she could feel his muscles bunching up tightly underneath his shirt.

Caydence moved her hands under his shirt and felt him clench his stomach when her fingers slid up slowly. He was just as affected by her presence as she was his. She found it extraordinary to know she had the same power over him that he had over her. He broke the kiss to lead her toward the bed. The closer they got to it, the more Caydence started to panic. If she did this, there was no turning back. But she already knew she would never go back. There was a lot to learn from him, and she would glean everything she could. Even if no one ever measured up to the masterpiece that was now just as naked as she was. When had that happened?

He lowered her carefully to the bed, and she could feel the strain in his body. Caydence knew he was trying to take it slow, but she didn't want that. She wrapped her arms around his neck and brought him closer to her. When his skin melded against hers, she knew real bliss. Hot, hard, hungry. That was how she wanted him, but she had no idea how to achieve that.

"If you're not careful, this will be over before it's begun," he cautioned her.

Would that be so wrong? Not that she didn't want all the rest of this, if it was going where she thought it would. When he ran kisses down her face to the base of her neck, she brushed her nipples against his chest and sighed softly. She felt like a kitten stretching from a long nap, and when his teeth caught her ear inside them, she almost pushed him off her.

"Oh!"

She felt him shake against her, and knew his control was weak at best. Caydence had been aching for him since the first time he had kissed her — she simply had not realized the signs at the time. "Please," she whispered.

He rose and ran a finger against her chin. "Please what, Caydence?"

Yes, what? What did she want? What words would make sense? The more he ran his fingers down her body, the more she wanted. "I ache for you."

He saw her nibbling her bottom lip and sucked in his breath. "Where?"

He was not going to put her out of her misery any time soon. He wanted to hear her say it. She felt the annoying blush take over again, and she felt it from her head to her toes. Caydence was so mortified she looked away.

"Don't be embarrassed, Caydence." His cock rubbed

against her leg and she moaned. "Is that what you want?"

"*Yes.*" It was a haunting whisper. Caydence thought she might die a thousand deaths if he made her wait here like this. She reached down and wrapped her hand around him. "*Please.*"

He groaned aloud and pumped into her hand a few times before he pushed away from her. Tyler foraged around near the top of the bed, where apparently he had stashed a few of the condoms from the honeymoon basket. He gave her a wicked grin. "Just in case."

She swatted his arm and shook her head at him. "Am I that predictable?"

"No. Not at all." His eyes lingered over her body, taking her in inch by inch. When he met her gaze again, they looked like liquid gold.

"Good. Can I?" She licked her lips and waited for him to hand her the condom.

His eyebrow rose in surprise. "Be my guest."

Caydence opened the package and pulled it out. She slid the bottom over him and started to roll it slowly down. She watched the way he twitched beneath her, and bit her bottom lip. That was when he took over. He quickly rolled it down and pushed her gently back onto the bed.

"God, you're remarkable."

"I do talk a lot," she teased him.

"And I'm incorrigible," he answered her.

"Well, let me help you with that." Caydence opened her legs wide for him and pushed her hips up toward him. "Just a little encouragement."

He took her mouth in with a growl as he slid into her. Caydence felt herself stretch against him. Her insides shivered around him as she thought about how large and filling he was.

"You're so tight," he whispered in her ear.

Caydence whimpered. No one had ever whispered sweet anythings in her ear when they were rising and falling into her.

"Do you like that, Caydence?" His breath was so hot she thought her ears would incinerate on the spot.

"Yes!" She answered as she arched her back. Her nipples brushed against his chest, and she shivered in anticipation.

"God, you feel so good."

This time his words shook her to the core. With his cock stretching her to the limit, her hips started to have a mind of their own. Every time he plunged into her, she felt her temperature rise another notch. She wanted him more than the air she breathed, and as the storm built inside her, she found herself holding her breath, waiting for what she was not entirely sure.

"Breathe, Caydence," he ordered her as he continued to push into her.

When she let out a breath and took another in, she felt herself spiraling out of control. Her entire insides shook around him, a tiny flutter at first, followed by a raging wave she could not control.

He must have felt it too, for he shouted, "God, yes."

Caydence was still dazed and confused before she realized that Tyler had started breathing raggedly on top of her. His mouth captured hers and she arched against him. The remnants of his erection teased her slightly before he pulled out of her. When he moved away from the bed, she already missed his heat. She watched him clean himself off before he stood over the bed looking down at her.

"I knew I could make you blush from head to toe."

Caydence looked down at her body and realized he was speaking the truth. Her body was still hot and ready for him, but rather than push the issue, Tyler did something unexpected. He lay down next to her and pulled her against his body. She breathed in his scent and sighed as he stroked the skin on her back softly.

"He was definitely an idiot."

Caydence flinched slightly. Dalton did not belong in this time or space. She was about to say so, but she realized that he was complimenting her. "That was amazing."

"I still have plenty of tricks in my bag," he promised her.

"Oh?" She was suddenly very happy that she had chosen a two week cruise. She couldn't even begin to imagine anything better than what she had just had. "Like what?"

"Wouldn't you like to know?" he teased her.

"Yes...," she whispered against him. Caydence shivered when his hand ran against her chest. Her nipples were still very much erect.

"I think you'll just have to wait until later." He looked down at her and saw the look on her face. "You're adorable when you pout."

Caydence swatted him with her hand as a yawn worked its way out of her mouth. "Rogue."

"Are you tired, Caydence?"

"No...." Another yawn and her eyes started to feel heavy. She stretched her body, rubbing against his softly. She hated to admit it, but exhaustion had started to settle into her bones. He held her close as she drifted off to sleep, with his small chuckle acting as a lullaby.

Chapter 12

When Caydence next awoke, the sheets were cold next to her. How long had she been asleep? Where was Tyler? She looked around the room and did not see him anywhere. Stretching deliciously, Caydence was like a cat waking from a delicious nap. She couldn't believe she had fallen asleep in his arms. When was the last time that had happened to her? Caydence couldn't actually remember ever being so sexually satisfied that she curled up in a sleepy coma afterwards.

She pushed away from the bed and stood up. As she walked around the room, she felt a slight chill. Looking down, she realized she was still completely naked. Not one to walk around with no clothes on, she looked for her shirt. When she did not see it near her, she grabbed the nearest garment. Tyler's shirt. She held it up to her face and smiled as his cologne drifted up to her nose. Sliding it over her head, she was surprised to see it went midway down her thighs.

Caydence walked over to the balcony and saw the moon was high in the sky. The round orb reflected on the water below and the light shimmered across the waves. It was....

"Breathtaking," Tyler whispered.

Her breath caught in her throat as she turned to see him sitting in one of the loungers. So that was where he had gone to. She almost breathed a sigh of relief. Not that she owned him, but the thought of him out on the ship made her a little worried that some other woman would capture his interest. Not that Tyler reminded her of a homewrecker. She highly doubted he would want that kind of entanglement.

His eyes were traveling the length of her body before he stood up and walked over to her. She saw he was wearing only a pair of boxers. He moved so that he was only a foot away from her. "I think it looks better on you."

What? She couldn't even process what he was saying with him being so close to her, yet so far away. How had he managed to make her forget everything in the world just by his proximity? Her eyes met his, and she licked her bottom lip as she waited to see what he was going to do next. She saw something flash in his eyes, as if he was stuck in a thought he did not share. Caydence related to that. She had so many of her own that she never voiced. Like how much she wanted to feel alive in his arms again.

Inches. She moved herself closer to him. Centimeters. Reaching for him, she bridged the rest of the gap to his kiss. Wrapping her arms around his neck, she sighed against him as she felt his arms pull her closer. With every kiss he pulled her deeper in, and Caydence wasn't sure she could ever pull herself out.

When he broke the kiss, Caydence looked up at him through heavy lids. "Mr. Jensen, you are quite the kisser."

"As are you, Mrs. Jensen," he teased her.

"And what would you do, if this were our honeymoon?" Her words were out before she could retract them. Biting her lip, she turned away from him and tried to remind herself this was not that kind of situation. They may pretend that they were married outside of these walls, but Caydence was not going to fool herself.

"I would make sure you knew how beautiful you are." He put a hand on her chin and pulled her face back to his.

Caydence sighed against him as his mouth moved over hers. He pulled her against him, cradling her as if she were the most precious thing in the world. Caydence felt every inch of her worries drift on the wind as his mouth moved down her face to the curve of her neck. The world was silent, with only the gentle hum of the ship's motors, which seemed to be drowned out by the fiercely beating heart that echoed in the darkness.

When his hands worked under the shirt, Caydence sucked in her breath and Tyler's tongue slipped into her mouth. He moved the shirt up and almost growled when he found she was not wearing anything underneath. Caydence felt him stiffen next to her, and she smiled in triumph. Clearly, she affected him as much as he did her.

As he lifted the shirt up, Caydence broke the kiss. "What are you doing, Tyler?"

"Ravishing my wife." He winked at her and her breath caught in her throat as he completely removed the shirt.

Wife? Oh God, the idea made her insides throb. How was that possible? Then a thought broke through the haze. "Tyler,

101

someone might see."

"Let them." His mouth devoured her neck.

Caydence threw her head back and tried to come up with any rational thought to make him stop. The problem was, she didn't want him to. The very idea that someone could see her standing there in all her naked glory should make her feel embarrassed from head to toe. Tyler did not make her feel that way though. With just one touch, one glance, one kiss, he made her feel like the most beautiful woman in the world.

She was so distracted that she didn't even notice him moving her back toward the loungers. Tyler sat down on the chair, and when she thought he was going to pull her down with him, his hands turned her around so that she was no longer facing him. Then he lowered her down to his lap. His hands moved up her stomach as his mouth moved against her back. The combination almost made her buck herself off his lap.

"Relax, Caydence."

His breath at her ear made her whimper slightly. She had the idea that he was much better at this than she had first thought. Much better. Every touch turned the heat up another notch, and when his fingers tweaked against her nipples, Caydence thought she was going to lose her mind.

"Tyler," she moaned. He stiffened under her and his hands drifted lower. Her stomach muscles bunched up when he passed her belly button. She ground herself against him and felt his erection growing strong between them.

"Caydence," he whispered in her ear. She loved the way her name sounded on his lips. It was like no other woman in the world existed, not in this moment in time. She refused to think of how many might be on the outside world somewhere. Tonight, she belonged here in his arms.

His hand dipped lower, and when his fingers started to massage her clit, Caydence almost jumped.

"What are you doing?"

"Ravishing you in the moonlight." When he sensed her resistance, he whispered, "Relax, Caydence."

When his fingers continued to rub against her, she felt something growing inside her. A mad longing filled her as his fingers brought her to a feverish pitch. With his other hand kneading her breast, his finger strumming against her, and his mouth moving against her back, Caydence was filled with a need she had never felt before. She did not think of him in that moment, only of capturing the bliss that was rising inside her and releasing it into the open air. She rode his fingers, worked her hips up and down, mimicking the one thing she wanted more than anything right now, to feel the length of him stretched out inside her.

The more he worked her over, the harder it was for her to think. As the first orgasm ripped through her, Caydence felt electrified. Like a bird freed from its cage, her moans carried on the wind and echoed around her. She thought he would stop, but he did not. Instead, he continued the course, refusing to let the languid pleased feeling settle over her. The calm she craved was out of reach, and in its place a frenzy started to build. She could not fight this feeling even if she tried. She felt him grind himself into her bottom, the only barrier the briefs that covered him.

"I want you dripping," he whispered in her ear.

Caydence nearly lost her mind. She had never wanted anyone, anything, like she did him in this moment in time. When his finger slipped inside her, she writhed against him. "Oh, yes."

His finger moved deep inside her, and she pushed against it. She rode it, the way she wanted to ride his cock, but he refused to give that to her. Caydence rocked up and down, panting and whimpering, for the release she wanted was so deliciously close to the surface. When she shook against him, she felt him strain behind her.

"Yes, cum for me, Caydence. God, yes."

She bit her lip to trap the screams that wanted to break free. Caydence was mad for him as she continued to push against his hand. When he moved his hand and replaced it with his cock, Caydence's eyes flew open. She clenched around him and her breath caught in her throat. "Tyler...."

"Trust me, Caydence." His voice was near her ear, and God help her, she would do anything he asked. He was like her puppet master.

The heat of his engorgement seared her. She was so transfixed in the fantasy that was building around her. Like a bride on her honeymoon, she took every inch of him into her body, not worrying about the consequences of her action as the desire of the moment blanketed her. When he moved in and out at a deliciously slow pace, every inch of him was a tantalizing treat, her bottom slamming into him as she rode him. His hands stroked her breasts, and the heat of his body against her back nearly sent her over the edge.

"God, you feel so good, Caydence."

He was rewarded with a fresh wave of cream as his hands gripped her breasts. She bucked against him, her insides shivering against his heat. He stiffened and tried to reign himself in.

"We have to stop, Caydence."

But to stop would kill her. She wanted every inch of him, and whatever came with it. Moving up and down the length of him, Caydence tried to draw him past his concerns.

"Caydence," he cautioned her.

"*Please…,*" she whispered, and heard the intake of his breath as he tightened against her.

"*Caydence.*" His voice was a whisper as he held himself transfixed on the brink.

"*Please…let me feel all of you.*" She had never wanted anything more than to feel him cum inside her, and by the way he gripped her breasts, he wanted that too.

When she pulled up and pushed back down on him, she felt his resolve shatter. He started to pump into her as his hand squeezed against her tight nipples. The gentle kisses on her back turned to sharp nibbles as he started to devour her flesh. The tempo between them rose, and Caydence felt another orgasm starting to form.

"Come on, Caydence, let go."

She shivered as he drove into her over and over. When she could no longer hold back, she fell back against him, letting herself go. As she quivered around him, Tyler's body went taut behind her. "God, yes, cum for me, Caydence."

She felt a warmth fill her core, and she shivered in

anticipation as he bucked into her three more times. Her excitement rose and she rode the length of him a few more times, before she finished once more. As she sat there, with him still inside her, she felt his cock pulsing. She had never had a man stay in her in the aftermath of the lovemaking. The way he twitched made her feel powerful. She clenched around him and he growled.

"Minx," he whispered in her ear.

"Mmmmm...." She had really enjoyed that. "Can we do that again?"

He jerked inside her and flicked her nipples with his fingers. "Perhaps later."

Caydence sighed as he slid out of her. He pulled her into his arms and she sat against him. This was what it should feel like to be loved. To be on a honeymoon with her husband. Was it so wrong that she could easily see him as Dalton's replacement?

After they finally caught their breaths, Tyler shifted against her. "Time to go in?"

"I guess." Caydence was almost disappointed. She could stay out here for eternity with him, naked in his arms.

Scooping up the shirt, she slid it back over her shoulders.

When Caydence walked into the room, she saw a tray of food on the table.

"How long has that been there?"

"I ordered it earlier, thinking you might be hungry when you woke up."

"I was," she answered ruefully.

He chuckled. "Insatiable. Just the way I like it."

She blushed as she sat down on the couch. Reaching over, she picked up one of the sandwiches. The crust was not as fresh as it would have been a few hours ago, but she didn't mind. She was actually famished, having worked off a lot of calories in a matter of minutes. Sex was definitely good cardio.

When she finished eating her food, Caydence was surprised to find that she was tired again. Had it really been that long of a day?

Tyler seemed to understand. He held a hand out to her. "To bed with you."

Caydence pouted slowly. She didn't want the moment to end, but clearly she was not in any state to continue any kind of physical activity right now. She stood up, ready to walk, but he scooped her up in his arms.

"What are you doing?"

"Putting my *wife* to bed." His eyes had a merry twinkle in them.

Caydence snuggled into his neck and let her mind continue with the fantasy. When he carefully lowered her to the bed, he followed it up with soft kisses to each of her eyelids. He climbed in beside her and pulled her into his arms. She curled against him, having never felt this loved and satisfied in her life. Afraid for what tomorrow would bring, she wanted to live transfixed in this moment in time. Would that be so terrible? She knew she did not know him that well, but her heart was his if he wanted it. Caydence would not kid herself. The first show of concern, the first brush of his lips against hers, and she had belonged to him.

Chapter 13

The next day, they spent the majority of the day near the poolside. Caydence particularly enjoyed nuzzling up against him in the hot tub. He had not seemed to mind either, as his fingers dipped underneath her bottoms. Caydence had to fight an orgasm off with at least two other couples in the tub with them. Her insides still throbbed from lack of completion.

Right now, they were back in the cabin stretched out deliciously on the bed together. She was still in her bikini when she climbed on top of him. "Ready to pick up where we left off earlier?"

"I wish, but we have other duties to attend to."

"Duties? What duties?" His words confused her.

"We have a captain's dinner."

"What?" She almost flew up in bed.

"Didn't you see the card earlier?" He stroked her arm absently.

What card? What was he talking about? She took a deep breath and tried to focus on his words. Then she remembered that the meal was part of the honeymoon package. "Right.

Fancy dinner."

"Maybe we should have him make it official," he suggested.

She punched him playfully on the chest. "Don't joke about that."

"Who's joking?"

Caydence was speechless. How in the world could he be saying something like that? "I barely know you."

"And yet...." He gestured to her nearly naked body straddling him.

And just like that, the spell was broken. She moved away from the bed and started to gather her clothes. Caydence was halfway to the closet when his hands pulled her against him. Emotions swirled inside her, and she turned to face him. Her hands swung out at him, and he let her take her rage out on him. When she realized she was pummeling his chest, tears started to fall down her face. "I'm sorry. I don't know why I did that."

"I can take it, Caydence." His voice was understanding. "I didn't mean to make light of marriage."

Her eyes met his. "I know. That's not something I want right now."

"Then we'll keep up our charade. A little role play never hurt anyone." He grinned at her, but his eyes spoke a different story entirely. It was as if her denial had cut him to the core.

But they barely knew each other. Why would her words hurt him? She was missing a piece to the puzzle, she was sure of it. She couldn't help thinking she had made a horrible mistake. Sex. That was what she was after. It was the only way

109

she was going to make it through this infernal couple's cruise when everyone was so head over heels for each other. Even the older people seemed to have their faces stuck together everywhere she looked.

"We'll just keep up pretenses."

"And when we're here?" he asked her.

"Whatever happens in Vegas...."

"I've never been to Vegas."

Caydence didn't know what he meant by that. That he couldn't pretend, or that he had never actually been to Vegas? Did it matter? She'd never been to Vegas herself, nor had she pretended to be married to someone. Engaged, yes. She realized that now. Dalton had never been truly engaged to her. Not the way she had been to him.

Tyler walked over and pulled her into another earth shattering kiss. She looked up at him in confusion. "What was that for?"

"I'm in Vegas. I might as well." He winked at her and went to gather his clothes to get dressed.

Vegas, my ass, she thought to herself. He was being... incredibly distracting? Caydence took a deep breath and looked for a spare towel. While he had showered this morning, she had not. Mostly because she did not want him staring at her while she showered. Now, she no longer cared. Let him take his turn. Maybe it would distract him from his harebrained notion that they should get married.

As Caydence worked on her hair and makeup, her mind kept turning back to his words. Why in the world would he ask her to marry him? It didn't make any sense to her at all. They had barely known each other two days, and even though he made her heart race more than any other man had, she didn't see how she could even begin to consider that proposal. Was it in the heat of the moment? Surely he had not been serious.

By the time she was ready, she found him staring at her. Caydence started to feel a little self-conscious as she pushed her brown hair behind her ears. She looked in the mirror and could not see what he was so transfixed on. "Do I have something in my teeth?"

"No." He grinned. "Not at the moment. Am I supposed to tell you if you do?"

"Good Lord! Yes!"

"You had spinach in your teeth earlier," he teased her.

"I did not!" She knew he was just teasing her, but she felt like throwing something at him. Picking up the first thing she could, she tossed it at him.

He held her panties in his hands and his eyebrows rose curiously. "Going commando?"

"What?" She felt the familiar heat rush to her face. Good grief! Caydence walked over to retrieve them.

"Ah-ah." He held a hand up. "Vegas, remember?"

She crossed her arms in front of her and felt her nose crinkle. "Tyler!"

"Come here." He held them up for her to slide into, but as his hands slid up her legs, his lips followed.

"If you keep that up, we're going to be late," she warned him.

"It's our honeymoon. They're probably used to it." His hand delved into the folds between her legs. When his finger tweaked against her clit, Caydence's knees nearly buckled.

"Tyler! Stop. I'm actually hungry."

"Pity. So am I." He slid the band around her stomach, then rose from the bed.

Caydence walked over to him and kissed him on the cheek. "Rain check?"

"Without doubt." He slapped her ass with his hand.

"Hey!"

"I would have preferred commando. Then I could have slid my hands up your legs all night."

Caydence straightened her white chiffon dress around her legs and grabbed his arm. "Play nice, Tyler."

"Oh, I can be nice. I can be *real* nice." He winked at her.

"That I don't doubt."

"Shall we?"

Caydence tried to prepare herself for the dinner they were about to share. What were they going to talk about? Why in the world had she scheduled that? Status, that's right. It was something Dalton had wanted added to their package. He wanted to be able to boast about sitting at the captain's table. Well, that had surely bit her in the ass now, hadn't it?

As they were welcomed to the table, she found it was not as awkward as she thought it would be. There were simple niceties shared with the other couples. She was starting to feel a little less out of place until the captain interrupted the conversation.

"So, tell us how you all met." He was nice enough looking man, with a puffy cheeked smile that reminded her a lot of her grandfather.

Caydence looked over at Tyler, like a deer trapped in headlights. She quickly tried to come up with an answer to that. Maybe they should have discussed it.

"Actually, we're not married."

"Oh, I was led to believe that you were in the honeymoon cabin."

Caydence wanted to hide under the table. Why had he just said that? She wanted to take her fork and stab him in the knee for that.

"Yet. I keep trying to get her to marry me. Ever since the moment I saw her in the elevator."

Elevator? What nonsense was he spinning right now? His words were so convincing she almost believed them.

"That day, I promised I would never see her cry again."

Her eyes met his and she felt some connection she had not realized. "Tyler, surely they don't want to hear all about that."

"Her fiancé had just ripped her heart out of her chest, cheating ass. I've been looking for her ever since. Imagine my luck when he offered to sell me his tickets." His voice seemed to catch in his throat.

"Aww, how romantic."

"And stalkerish," Caydence threw in half-heartedly. She wasn't afraid of him. Maybe she should be, because how many men would follow a stranger halfway around the world to try to…. What…seduce them? She was sure there was also some other pieces she had not quite heard.

Tyler chuckled. "I'm harmless."

"Well, that sounds a little like destiny," one of the ladies

113

almost swooned on the table.

Caydence reached for his hand and squeezed it, perhaps a little harder than she intended at first, but no one but Tyler seemed to notice.

He cleared his throat. "Eh hem. Excuse us. Care for a dance?"

A dance? After what he'd just said, she was afraid to be near him. How did she respond to that? His eyes pleaded with her, and Caydence relented. She allowed him to lead her to the dance floor. Caydence was glad no eyes seemed to be fixed on them. "Have you lost your mind?"

"Perhaps," he answered her. His eyes were unreadable.

"You followed me here?" Caydence barely remembered him being in the elevator. Her mind had been pretty occupied that day.

"I wasn't certain you would actually be here, but I hoped." He cleared his throat. "I knew your pain. I've been hurt too."

Caydence looked up at him, and knew that every word he spoke was true. "Are you going to hurt me?"

"Not if I can help it."

"You're not a stalker for real, are you?"

"No. Are you a ghost?" He countered.

"Why?" she asked him.

"Because your face has haunted me ever since."

Caydence broke away from his embrace and started to walk out onto the balcony. She needed air, she needed to think. One glance, and he had been willing to follow her all the way here. The warning bells were missing. Why weren't they ringing in her head? It was actually the most romantic gesture anyone had ever done, even if slightly unhinged.

What did she do now? Things had changed. They always did, way too fast for her to reason with sometimes. One moment she was engaged and seemingly happy. The next her heart was smashed into a million pieces on the elevator floor. Before she knew it, she was in handsome stranger's arms as if by chance. Now, she knew chance did not factor into it at all. Chance was a fickle creature.

"Caydence...," his voice called to her.

She ignored him and continued to stare out at the water. The moon was haunting and beautiful, and she could easily get swept away with the romance of it all, but Caydence had enough experience with heartache to know she wasn't quite ready to head down that path again.

"My fiancé cheated on me too." His words were soft at first. "I thought I would never get over that. Never find a woman who made me want to feel again. The moment I saw your face in the elevator, I wanted to save you from the pain."

"It isn't your job."

"No...but I want it to be."

"I don't need anyone to save me." Her voice was bitter now. Why was it that everyone thought she couldn't think for herself? First, Dalton had refused to let her plan the wedding.

She couldn't even look at Tyler. Without knowing it, he had stolen a piece of her, just as Dalton had. His omission was nearly as bad as the lie that Dalton had told. Although, Dalton was the one who had cheated on her. She turned to face Tyler and saw the emotions clouding his face. "No more lies, Tyler."

"No more lies." His words were like a soft promise.

"Separate beds." It was the only wall she could throw between them that would make her feel like she had the upper hand.

"If that's the way you want it."

It wasn't the way she wanted it, but a wall had been drawn between them, and she was not about to retract it any time soon. Earlier she had felt like a different person, someone who could possibly be happy. Now, she was back to square one—numb, vulnerable, and lost. If she were going to survive this cruise, she would have to learn how to ignore him. Unfortunately, she knew that would be like ignoring the very air she breathed. Maybe she could find a way back home sooner.

Caydence walked away from him, leaving him at the balcony. She wasn't sure how this had gone to hell so quickly. That was probably the fastest relationship she had ever had. Considering how fast she had jumped into bed, it was easy to see it was doomed from the start. That was just her luck, apparently.

Chapter 14

When she made it back to the room, she quickly changed into the night clothes that covered more of her body. She pulled a blanket out and made her bed on the couch. As she lay there, she wondered where he could be. Was he coming back? Did she want him to?

In the time that he had been gone, her mind had gone in so many different directions. Would it have been so bad if he had chased her out of the building to check on her? To have pursued her in town? Not really. She would not have accepted his attention then, but it would have been less creepy. There was something else she was fighting too. In two days, her feelings were stronger for him than any other man she had known before. Caydence wasn't even sure how that was possible. Honestly, it was crazy, right? Yet here she sat, more worried about him coming back than if he were here. She wanted him here, no matter how strange or crazy that might seem. Maybe she needed her life to be shaken up.

It was nearly two in the morning when she heard the click of the lock. She sat up and looked toward the door.

"Sorry, I didn't mean to wake you," he apologized.

"You didn't," Caydence answered him.

"I can take the couch if you want," he offered.

Caydence stood up and turned the lights on dim. His eyes looked a little strained. Had he been drinking? Why hadn't she thought of that? If ever there were a time she wanted to be plastered, tonight might be one of those nights. She saw the worry on his face and she wanted to chase it away.

"Tyler, can we talk?"

"Talk?" He looked confused. "You still want to talk to me?"

Caydence sighed. She had gone off the rails at him a little. "Have a seat."

He moved slowly toward her, almost as if he didn't trust himself to sit down next to her. "I've been trying to find another cabin. A helicopter, anything to make this right."

"No!" Her word came out stronger than she intended. Caydence did not want him to leave.

"I acted selfishly."

"Yes, you did," she agreed.

He looked hurt by her words, but he didn't say a thing.

She took his hand in hers. "But I forgive you."

"Why?"

"I wish I knew."

She didn't know what else to say. There was no real explanation that fit. It wasn't like she was head over heels for him. She barely knew him, but she wanted to. The real him. The one who had talked about her so passionately before. That man was worth knowing. No one had shown that much compassion for her before.

"So…you want me to stay." He looked as if he were trying to figure out what that meant.

Caydence was trying to figure that out too. All those years with Dalton, she wished she would have followed her instincts. If she had been honest with herself, Caydence had known for some time that he was not the right man for her. The only thing she wanted to do was smooth the worry from Tyler's face. She wasn't sure where that emotion came from, but she wanted to know more about it. If she ended up devastated in the end, at least she would feel like she was living.

"I do."

She reached out to touch his face and closed her eyes. She did not know what to say to him right now. Caydence wasn't even sure the words existed. Letting her hand slide over his face, she felt his lips under her fingertips. She heard his intake of breath and slid closer to him.

"What are you doing, Caydence?"

"I dunno." It was true. She had no idea what she was doing. Her heart and brain were at complete odds with each other.

He jerked his head away in reflex and ran a hand through his hair. "I don't know what you want me to do here, Caydence. One minute you're ready to toss my ass overboard, and now you're…. Well, I'm not certain what you are."

She felt tears line her eyes. "Neither am I."

"Oh hell. Don't cry." He pulled her into his lap and stroked her head.

Caydence felt safe in his arms, but she wanted something else entirely. She didn't want to feel safe. Caydence wanted to feel loved, but how did she ask for that? Maybe the best route was direct communication. "Will you...?"

"Anything. You name it," Tyler answered her, and she could tell he meant it.

"Make love to me."

She felt him stiffen beneath her. "Caydence...."

"Please. I just want to know — "

She did not even get to finish her words. His mouth covered hers in a kiss that was so soft and sweet, Caydence thought she might start crying all over again. She wanted to know what it felt like to have a man hold her in his arms and make her feel like she was the center of his universe. Passion was one thing, but anyone could be passionate. Loving, that was so much harder to do. If he had any kind of feelings for the woman he thought she was, shouldn't he be able to do that?

His hand brushed over her ear and held her head up so that he could rain kisses down her face. He nuzzled her nose with his own. Wrapping his arms around her, he lifted her from the couch and carried her to the bed. He carefully removed her clothing and followed it with his own. Then he lay next to her and held her in his arms.

"Tyler...," she whispered. Caydence wanted more than this.

"Patience, Caydence."

His hand moved down her skin, slowly caressing her side as his mouth started to memorize her face with kisses that were so light, she almost thought she imagined them. While she lay there naked in his arms, Caydence felt a slow sensuous heat rising inside her. He did not rush the moment, more intent on making her feel cherished than taking what his body wanted. This was about her.

Tyler continued to move down her body, his mouth taking in every inch. When his tongue circled her nipple, Caydence whimpered softly. His mouth pulled her in and sucked her softly. Caydence wrapped her hands in his hair and pulled him closer, as if she wanted him to swallow her whole. He released her and repeated the process with her other breast.

Caydence felt like she was floating on a cloud. The more flesh his mouth took in, the higher she started to rise. When his mouth settled between her legs, her eyes shot open. His tongue snaked against her clit and she moaned softly. He stirred the fires gently building up a slow inferno inside her. She came against him as the slow desire continued to trickle through her. When he sucked her clit into his mouth, she gripped the sheets and almost bucked him off her. The desire changed inside her in a flash.

She wanted any tangible piece of him, for now, for later, forever. Tears fell down her face when he brought her to the brink again and again. When he looked up at her, his eyes were filled with an adoration she did not think she deserved, yet she wanted it so badly.

Tyler moved up the bed and kissed the tears away from her face. When he moved her legs apart and slid inside her, she sighed softly. Her body welcome him with a silky sweetness that made her tremble around him. No matter how much his body strained against her, he kept his pace gentle and slow. Her insides quivered around him gently, like a butterfly who flew for the very first time. Caydence tried to hold on to the moment as long as she could, but the drive inside her changed too quickly. While he tried to keep the tempo slow and steady, Caydence kept pushing and pulling against him, wanting more than he was giving.

"Caydence," he cautioned her.

She brought his mouth down to hers and caught any other objections in a slow languid kiss. Her hips rose and fell, faster and faster, taking what she needed. He gave in to her demands, meeting each thrust with his own. She could barely breathe, she was so delirious with desire. When her orgasm finally rose to the surface, it collided with his own.

Caydence lay there, her arms wrapped around him, pulling him closer into her embrace. She could feel the rise and fall of his breath as he tried to steady the same emotions that were racing through her. She threw caution to the wind and whispered, "Yes."

He rose up to look her in the eye. "Yes?"

"I think I will marry you." She said it before she could retract it.

He closed his eyes and let out a slow sigh. When he opened them, they were filled with an emotion she could not read. "I don't deserve you."

Caydence smiled and ran her hand against his face. "I'm not sure how you did it."

"What?" He kissed the palm of her hand and grinned when she flinched.

"Made me fall for you."

"You have to say it, Caydence." He looked as if he were waiting for his fate to be decided at his own personal trial.

"I love you."

He sucked in his breath and lowered his mouth to hers in a hungry kiss. Her words had stirred more than his emotions. His erection started to twitch inside her. She clenched around him and moaned against him. Even though she longed to hear those words repeated, she could not resist the urge to pull him in deeper.

This time he rode her long and slow as his tongue dueled hers for control. A longer ride for sure, for his stamina had returned. "God, you feel so good."

"Mmmmm...," she moaned as her insides sucked him in further. They stayed there forever, it seemed, trapped in a moment she would never forget for the rest of her life.

When he came inside her again, he called out her name. "Caydence!"

As their breathing stilled, he put his hands on each side of her face and kissed her softer than she'd ever been kissed before. Then he whispered something no one had ever truly said to her. "I love you."

Not even Dalton had been able to make her feel this kind of truth. Without a doubt, Caydence snuggled against him feeling like the most fortunate woman to walk to the earth. As she fell asleep, her brain started to fire again. Wait...what did she just do? She tried to get her mind to focus on the reason for the panic rising up in her. Maybe she would remember tomorrow.

Chapter 15

When Caydence finally woke up, she found Tyler staring down at her. "What are you doing?"

"Staring at an angel."

She rolled her eyes. After last night, she certainly did not feel like any angel. "What time is it?"

"Noon." He grinned at her.

"It is not!" She picked up a pillow and hit him with it.

"You can assault me all you like, but that won't change the truth," he teased her.

"Oh my goodness. Why didn't you wake me up?"

"You looked like you needed the sleep." He brought his lips down to hers and kissed her softly.

What was supposed to be an innocent kiss turned into something quite different, for the moment he came closer, she remembered the sweet lovemaking from the night before. Her nipples rose at the memory and scraped deliciously against his chest.

He pulled away and narrowed his eyes on her. "Haven't you had enough yet?"

She licked her lips. "The day is just starting."

"You're insatiable." He teased her with his words and his fingers as he flicked them lightly over her nipple.

Caydence whimpered in reflex. "Can you dare deny me?"

"No...," he whispered as his hand slipped between her legs.

Her clit throbbed in anticipation. As he worked it over softly, one of his other fingers slid inside her. Her body stretched and she arched into him. He lowered his mouth to hers and she wrapped her arms around his neck. She sighed against him when his skin ran against her nipples. Caydence was already dripping and ready for him.

"You're so wet," his hot breath whispered in her ear.

Caydence nearly bucked his hand away as she came undone. He released her and plunged deep into her, riding the wave and pushing it further and faster.

"Yes, oh, yes."

"That's it, Caydence. Keep going...yes...oh, you feel so good."

So did he, like velvet and silk, as she wrapped her legs around him. He pushed her to oblivion and she took him with her. They were both panting by the time it was over.

She looked up at him and saw his disappointment. "What's wrong?"

"I'm weak." He gave her a sinful grin.

"I'm intoxicating," she teased him.

"Like a drug," he replied as he pushed into her one last time.

She whimpered. "Tease!"

"Maybe later, Caydence. Every man has his limits, darling."

When she raked her nails against his back, she felt his cock throb against her leg. She gave him a wicked grin. "Too bad women don't."

"Apparently not, but we'll have to explore that later, I'm afraid. You'll be raw if we keep this up." His eyes were filled with concern, and she sighed.

"You are truly remarkable, sir."

"Incorrigible?"

"That too, but I'm not helping, am I?"

"No, you're awfully encouraging. We'll get back to that. Now, get up, woman. I'm hungry."

"I could eat," she added. Although the feast she had in mind had nothing to do with food.

"Okay, now I'm starting to feel like a buffet." He held up his hands when she licked her lips. "Caydence...."

"Maybe later."

She sure hoped so. And she wasn't nearly as sore as he thought she was, probably because her body had been well lubricated before he plunged into her. Climbing out of bed, she went to use the restroom. Turning on the shower, she waited for the water to heat up. When she saw the steam inside, she climbed inside it. She sighed as the water cascaded down her back. She was halfway through washing her hair when she felt his hands slide around her body. His lips trailed kisses down her back.

"Mmm...thought you were done."

"He has a mind of his own. You'll have to take it up with

him," he whispered in her ear.

Her insides turned to hot lava as she thought about having a conversation with the cock that was standing at attention behind her. She relaxed against him when his soap filled hands rubbed against her stomach. When they slid over her chest, she shivered against him. Her hips moved and she teased his cock with her behind.

He groaned against her. "I'm feeling incorrigible."

"Oh?" She whispered. She turned around to face him, and his mouth was on hers faster than she could think. Caydence broke the kiss, even though she was enjoying it. She held a hand up and pushed him away from her. Sliding down the length of him, she saw his cock twitch in front of her.

"What are you doing, Caydence?" His voice sounded a little hoarse when she licked the tip of his cock.

"Encouraging you."

"I don't actually *need* much encouragement." He flinched when she pulled him into her mouth. He gripped the sides of the shower and his whole body tightened above her. "Oh God, now what are you…?"

Caydence was now nibbling his flesh as she teased it in her mouth. "Whatever I want. I am in Vegas, after all."

"God, I'm really starting to wish I'd visited sooner."

Caydence pulled her mouth away. "Me too."

This time, she let her tongue swirl around him. She slipped even lower and drew one of his balls into her mouth. With the hot steamy water flowing down around her, she was driven with a need she did not understand. She had never been this wild before. Her hands wrapped around to squeeze his ass as

127

she took the length of him into her mouth again.

"*Caydence….*" He strained against her as if trying to fight against the pleasure and pain ripping through his body. She felt his need, wanted to give him the release he craved. He was just on the brink, and she could feel it. Caydence loved the power she had over him, but he pushed her head away from him. His breathing was ragged as he ran a hand through his wet hair. "Come here."

Her eyebrow rose curiously, as if she could not understand what else he would want right now. She looked back at his engorged member and licked her lips. His eyes were on her when she looked up at him. "No."

She refused to do what he told her. She wasn't afraid of him. There was no consequence that would be any more damaging than refusing to let her continue. She had always wanted to know what it felt like to suck a man dry. Her mouth wrapped around him, and when he tried to pull away, she bit him.

"God!" His word came out in a clench.

Caydence wanted to bring him to the brink. Her hands rolled his balls around as she pulled him hard into her mouth. Like a newborn suckling a teat, she was hungry for just one taste of him. He was thrashing wildly under her mouth, finally giving in to her control. She knew she was denying her own needs, for her insides throbbed painfully, but she would not change this moment for anything else in the world. Caydence felt him tighten above her, and imagined the pure ecstasy that was etched on his face as his orgasm ripped through him. She took him in, sucking as hard as she could, and when his heat filled her mouth, she swallowed it whole.

His legs were shaking, but Caydence refused to let him go. Her hunger for him defied all the odds. She felt him twitch and she reluctantly pulled away. Caydence stood up and found her own legs shaking. She could not look at him, for part of her was starting to feel as if she had gone too far.

"Caydence, don't pull away." His words coaxed her.

Her eyes flew to his and she saw a blinding light inside the golden pools. Love. She stepped into his arms and let him hold her tightly. She sighed in contentment. "I've never—"

"I know."

"How was—?"

"If you finish that sentence, I am going to lose my mind. You are perfection, Caydence. From top to feisty bottom."

Caydence stepped away from him, and was about to leave the shower when he pulled her back to him.

"Where are you going, Caydence?"

"I thought we were—"

"Done? We're just getting started." His eyes looked as if he were going to devour every inch of her.

"But…." He had finished twice. It was less than likely he would be able to go for round three, wasn't it?

"Relax, Caydence. Let me love you."

Love. She shivered. Was that the same thing as desire? Because if it was, her entire body thoroughly loved him. His hands ran down her breasts, brushing against her nipples, and she arched against him. His mouth ran down her neck, licking the water droplets away. He continued lower, until his mouth perched between the small curls that rested between her legs.

"Open for me, Caydence." His hand slid beneath her legs as he parted her. He stuck his fingers inside her as his mouth sought her clit.

He spent the next few moments teasing her with his tongue as his fingers moved deep inside her. Her hips rode against him until she thought she would lose her mind. Her climax shattered around her, and she heard his intake of breath as he continued to pleasure her. Over and over he took her, and all the while Caydence tried to keep her balance as her legs threatened to buckle under her.

When she finished again, she heard the water turn off. He scooped her wet body in his and opened the door. Carrying her across the room, he tossed her on the bed. He was on her before she could think. Plunging deep inside her, Tyler took every inch of her. She had yet to see him this worked up, but it thrilled her. For the next half hour he plundered her depths, clearly aroused, but not ready to find his release. She lost track of her orgasms as he took every inch of her. As he crashed into her once last time, Caydence thought she was going to pass out. The lights floated behind her eyes as she came around him.

"Incorrigible," she teased him.

"Highly. But I do think I've had my limit." He grinned at her.

She surely hoped so. Any more and she would never be able to walk again. Her legs were already wobbly, and she hadn't even stood up yet. Snuggling into his arms, she sighed in contentment.

"Don't you dare fall asleep. I'm still hungry, and you've

already made me miss breakfast."

"Fine. Let's get food, but you might have to carry me," she teased him.

Chapter 16

When they made their way to the lunch buffet, Caydence felt more content than she had in quite some time. It was as if a load of stress had been lifted from her shoulders. Had it been that long since she'd actually just had fun? Enjoyed life? Lived a little? She marveled at how easy it was to walk with him, holding his hand in the simple silence of the moment. Uncomplicated, yet still so immensely complicated at the same time, considering what she had learned yesterday.

Tyler, broodingly handsome, had traveled halfway across the world just to see her. All he had known about her was the fact that her fiancé had been a dick and broken her heart. Knight in shining armor complex? Perhaps. But in so many ways she found that an attractive feature. He was already working harder on this relationship than most men in her world had up until this point. Yes, she did love him. As odd and suspect as that felt, she knew it was true. Every inch of her wanted all of him, and not just because he was spectacular in bed.

As they neared the doorway to the buffet, he lifted her

hand up and kissed it, before releasing it and gesturing for her to go first. Her eyes met his and she saw something guarded inside. It made her pause for a minute, but she shook it off. Gathering enough sustenance to get her through the rest of the afternoon, she found two seats and sat down to wait for him.

When the couple they had seen the day before approached her, Caydence tried not to groan. Did they have to intrude on their moment? Caydence wanted him all to herself, as greedy as that sounded. She also did not want to be responsible for all the questions they would send her way. Even so, she graciously nodded when they asked to sit down.

"Caydence, right?" Alice asked her.

"Yes, Alice?"

"Yep. And George here."

"I'm usually the forgettable one," he teased with a merry smile.

"Oh, stop. That's not true." Alice put her hand on his. "I think you're amazing."

"Even after five years of me?" He chuckled.

Caydence watched them with a little envy. What would it be like to be married to someone and happy even after a handful of years? To feel the love not only remain, but flourish? Did it make her foolish to want that kind of relationship with someone? She had thought to have it with Dalton. He had thought about having it with every skirt that walked past him. Clearly, he had issues that she had never realized before. As far as she knew, he could have been cheating all along.

"Ah. There's the hubs." Alice smiled at him.

Caydence felt her heart flutter slightly and looked down at her food. She tried to ignore the flush that was starting to rise up her face. When she looked over at Tyler, she found him smirking at her, as if he realized he was the cause for her discomfort.

"Where's your ring?" Alice broke through the moment.

Caydence almost dropped her fork and took a drink of water. Almost stuck in the moment, she tried to latch onto any idea that would keep her out of the spotlight at the moment. She stared at her finger and sighed loudly. "Goodness, would you look at that? I must have left it off when I put my lotion on this morning. Good thing you got that thing insured."

"Yes, good thing." Tyler was clearly enjoying the exchange.

Caydence made a mental note to punish him for it later. No need to make fun of her mirth. "Although, it's not nearly as flashy as yours."

Alice held up her finger. "Right? I thought I was going to die when George slid this on my finger."

Caydence wrinkled her nose. "Blinding. I'm more of a simple girl myself. I do a lot of typing, so something that large would just get in the way."

Caydence looked over at Tyler, who looked even more thoughtful. What was going on in that head of his now? Turning back to her food, she started to eat some of her omelet. As she did, Alice started in with the questions. Caydence was starting to feel like she was getting the third degree.

"So, are you planning on having kids right away, or are you going to wait?"

Caydence nearly spit out her water, and felt her eyebrows furrowing as she took another drink. In fact, she drank so much she almost drained the glass. She felt Tyler's hands on her back, as if he noticed her discomfort.

"We haven't decided yet," Tyler offered.

"Oh. We've been trying for the past year."

George interrupted her. "Alice, not everyone needs to know all of that."

"What? I'm just making friendly conversation." Alice grinned at them. "I want two kids."

"Just two?" Tyler interjected.

"I'd be happy with just one," George added.

"George!" Alice chided him.

"Have you seen what it costs to send one kid to college?" He shook his head. "One is enough to pay for."

Caydence smiled. Watching them getting into all of this should be uncomfortable, with them being strangers, but Caydence was starting to find it amusing.

"I've been saving for that since I first started working," Tyler added to the conversation. "Just in case. You never know what the future will bring. Better to be prepared."

Caydence reflected on her own childhood. As an only child, she had always wondered what it would have been like to be surrounded by a large brood of people. Inside, she had always wanted a large family, but she was already starting to feel like it was too late. "Me too. But I've always wanted lots of kids."

"Lots?" Tyler looked as if he were gulping slightly.

Caydence fought the urge to laugh aloud. Let him suffer

with that thought for a bit. "Well, more than one, less than ten. I'm too old to have that many."

"You don't look a day over twenty-three," Alice complimented her.

"Twenty-eight." She wrinkled her nose. "But I've got him convinced I'm only twenty-one."

"For the next twenty years. And when she hits fifty, she's only thirty-three. She's got the math down to a T. Good thing I'll always be five years older. She likes her men distinguished," Tyler teased.

Caydence sighed. None of this was true. Funny enough, they were learning more about each other than they had in the past few days. This had started off as an uncomfortable lunch, but she was starting to feel more comfortable by the minute. When his hand slipped behind her and started to rub her back, she smiled absently. She turned to look at him, and he leaned over to kiss her on the mouth. Just a small gentle kiss, and Caydence felt as if all the planets shifted their orbit to revolve around him. How in the world had he been single this long?

"Aww. So sweet." Alice reached for George's hand and the two of them held hands.

Yes, it was sweet. Innocent, for now at least. That was a good thing, considering how much her body still wanted to feel him working his magic on her. How was it possible to still feel so wet and ready? When his finger stroked the inside of her wrist, Caydence nearly yanked her hand away. She looked up at his knowing smile.

"So what are you going to do today?" Alice asked them

curiously.

Well, Caydence knew what they weren't going to do. At least not for a little while, but she didn't voice that. Although, she did start to wonder how many times a man could orgasm in one day. 'Cause honestly, she was starting to think he might have broken a world record already. Certainly more than any other man in her own experience. She started to realize that she was lacking serious education in that department. College men, yes, they had seemed to have more stamina, slightly more than a high school boy, who got too excited to really know how to use the equipment correctly.

"We haven't decided yet."

"Well, we're planning on spending some time at the pools, maybe try the surf pool. You're welcome to join us," offered Alice.

"Alice, it's bad enough that we have completely derailed their lunch. Remember our honeymoon?" He teased her.

"Oh, yes. We hardly left the room." She giggled and punched her husband on the shoulder when he gave her googly eyes.

"I'm sure we'll see you around," Caydence assured them. "And as you've guessed, I am rather insatiable for my husband."

Tyler seemed taken aback by her brutal honesty. He recovered and winked at her. "She hasn't let me leave her side."

"I sure do remember those days." Alice seemed almost envious.

"It was nice to see you again." Caydence gathered her

plate and cup and started to rise, but Tyler put his hand up.

"Let me get those, darling."

Darling? It was such an old term of endearment. Hon, honey, babe. Those seemed more common. Caydence watched him leave. "He's some kind of wonderful."

"Preach it, sister," agreed Alice.

"Well, see you." Caydence walked away from the table and immediately reached for his hand.

Tyler pulled her into his arms and kissed the top of her head. "I love how you don't pull away from me."

"I love how you always pull me closer." If they were going to start talking about all the things they liked, Caydence could start listing all the things he had already done that she liked. She brought her mouth up to his ears and whispered, "I'm still wet for you."

Tyler visibly flinched. "Woman, you're going to be the end of me."

Just like he was her beginning. She sighed when he hugged her tight to his chest. He wasn't aroused at the moment, which seemed like a cruel punishment for her to be the only one afflicted. Even now she could feel the pulse beating between her legs. It was all his fault for waking her up in ways she had never been. She was imagining how he could possibly top the past few days, and ached to find out as soon as possible.

"They're still watching," Tyler whispered to her.

"I figured." She snuggled against him, not caring about whatever audience might be watching her. She had never been one for public displays of affection, but it was growing on her. Whenever she was in his arms, there only seemed to be two people in her universe. It made her sad to think some people might go an entire lifetime without ever experiencing the feelings she was having in this moment in time.

The rest of the day started to move faster than Caydence wanted it too. She wanted to memorize every moment she was with him, because what may be here today could always be gone tomorrow. Anything that could be said in the heat of passion could disappear so quickly. The fact that they had not even talked about the small cloud hanging over them made her a little worried that she had imagined the night before.

When they walked by the video arcade, Caydence felt like squealing. "Look!"

"You like arcades?" He looked as if he were trying to figure out what kind of woman she was.

"I know it's silly, but it's the one thing I got to do with my dad. This was our thing." She smiled ruefully at him.

"Was?" he asked her quietly.

"I lost him when I was eighteen." It was ten years ago, but any time she walked near an arcade, she felt like he was still with her.

"I'm sorry to hear that. How did your mother take it?"

Caydence didn't answer right away. "I wouldn't know. She left when I was a baby. My dad and grandparents raised me. I took care of them for a while after I graduated."

Her voice was so matter of fact. Caydence had never really allowed herself to think about her circumstances. She felt that everything that had happened to her had helped build the woman she was. She looked up at him and saw him staring at her. "What?"

"You're an extraordinary woman."

"No, I'm not." Caydence waved his words away. She didn't want him to look at her like that. It made her feel all warm and fuzzy inside. Caydence much preferred the heat — for some reason that seemed so much safer.

Tyler let it slide. "Let's play then, shall we?"

"Oh, can we?" A smile lit up her face. She was half tempted to clap her hands excitedly.

He kissed her spontaneously. "I don't think I could deny you if I tried."

"Hmm…remind me to come up with a list, then." She winked at him and slapped him on the butt with her hand before walking away.

"Now who's being incorrigible?" he teased her.

For the next two hours they played every game in the arcade, some more than others. Caydence could not remember the last time she had laughed so hard, especially when she had challenged him to a dance battle. She had almost tripped over her own feet and knocked him off the game pad. Of course, he had accused her of cheating, which made it even more hysterical to her considering how horrible each of their scores were.

Tyler was turning in some of the tickets they had earned from some of the games. Caydence was still playing one of the shooting games when he returned. When her last life was over, she turned around to find him watching her with a smile. "What?"

He dropped down on his knees and held up a small toy ring before her. He was grinning outwardly, but she could see by the look in his eyes that he was not entirely sure what she would do. "Will you marry me?"

The cheesy sentimentality almost brought tears to her eyes. She would never forget this moment. He had already elicited a reply from her, but to do it here, where her father felt so close to her, it brought tears to her eyes. She knew he was smiling down on her from Heaven in this moment in time. "*Yes.*"

When he slid the plastic ring on her finger, she almost giggled. He gave her an apologetic smile. "I hadn't planned on all of this."

Caydence wiped a tear away. "Safe to say neither one of us did."

Tyler stood up and brushed away one of her tears before kissing her gently. "I love you, Caydence."

"I love you too." She lay her head on his shoulder.

So he did remember asking her. And she had said yes. As much as it had felt like fantasy rather than reality, here it was staring back at her, with its moldable metal band and the plastic pearl in the middle. Apparently, he was also paying attention to every word she said.

"I hope he would approve."

"My father always supported my choices, even when he struggled with them. Especially in my teenage years."

"You weren't a hell raiser, were you?" he teased her.

"I had my moments," Caydence giggled. "But they weren't nearly as wild as this vacation. Sleeping with a handsome stranger…that would never have happened."

"You called me handsome," he grinned at her.

"And sexy as hell."

His chest rumbled loudly as he chuckled. "I'll have to up my game if I'm going to keep you satisfied though, I think. Although, there are still plenty of things to try."

This time, she was the one who stiffened in his arms. The very idea of trying anything risqué with him made her shiver slightly. Why her mind went there, she had no idea. "I think you're teasing me."

"Maybe."

"Turnabout is fair play, Mr. Jensen," she warned him.

"Yes, yes, it is. I'm counting on it." His amber eyes had a wicked gleam to them. "But for now, I think you should get some rest."

"Rest?" Caydence pouted. That was the last thing her body wanted to do right now.

"You'll want some rest," he assured her with a wink.

"Oh...." She imagined them entertaining themselves on the balcony like they had the other night, and she closed her eyes to remember every aching detail.

"And what are you thinking about, Caydence?" His mouth asked her, its heat teasing her ears.

She sighed and felt her toes curling in her shoes. What was it about the way he whispered in her ear? She had never had sensitive ears before—or had she? Maybe he was just the first to discover it. "I'll never tell."

"We'll see about that."

Tyler led her back to their room, and while she thought he would spend a little more time stirring the desire within her, she was surprised to find herself cradled in his arms. She closed her eyes and let herself fall asleep to the rise and fall of his chest.

Chapter 17

Caydence was surprised to be alone in the cabin when she woke up. A slow smile spread across her face as she looked at the small ring that was on her finger. A child's toy, she knew, but she couldn't help but love every inch of it. Something so sweet and pure, it was not something she had ever expected from him. Tyler was clearly a romantic at heart. Stretching out, she saw the rose on her pillow.

"He's too good to be true." She saw a small note on her pillow.

Had a few things to do. I'll be back for dinner.

Dinner? Caydence looked at the clock and smiled. That would be anytime now. She got up from the bed and went to refresh herself. Considering a shower, she decided to wait and see if maybe he might join her later. Images of the last one were still tattooed on her brain. Heaven help her, Caydence might be the horniest woman on the planet. It wasn't her fault that he drove her delirious.

Thumbing through her clothes, Caydence pulled out one of her red dresses. She'd always loved this dress, but had

144

not really had a chance to use it. It was far too risqué for any of Dalton's dinner dates. With its low plunging neckline, it left very little to the imagination, and that was exactly what she was going for. The bodice was tight enough to keep her breasts trapped inside without needing a bra, even though she did have a strapless bra that would work. Feeling a little frisky, she decided to go without one. As she fingered her bottoms, a wry smile filled her face. The tight fitting skirt was long enough that she could get away with one last thing. She tossed the underwear back in the drawer and walked away.

Tyler was going to be in for quite some surprise — if he noticed, that was. Caydence sprayed one of her perfumes and closed her eyes. Whatever he had planned for the night, Caydence was more than ready for it. She sat down on the couch and crossed her legs to hide her lack of apparel underneath.

When the door opened, Caydence felt her heart skip a beat. "You're back."

"And you're already dressed."

"You look disappointed."

"I was hoping to help you." His grin was slightly wicked.

"Aww, poor baby." She stood up and walked over to soothe him with a kiss. "Are you ready to eat?"

"Starving," he whispered as he leaned down for a kiss. "You look ravishing."

"It's not too much?" she asked self-consciously.

"It could never be too much. Although, I'm not sure how I'm going to keep my hands to myself." He tried to move his hands to her behind, but her hands pushed him away.

Caydence did not want to give away the surprise. It was better for that to happen when he least expected it. She wondered what his response would be. She grabbed his hand. "I'm hungry — feed me, sir. I need more energy."

"For?" He pulled her closer and captured her mouth in a kiss. "Some of this?"

"Mmmm…yes, that would be nice. And some of this too." Caydence smacked his ass. "Now, stop messing around. Never get between a woman and a nice meal."

"Yes, ma'am."

His eyes were twinkling, as if he knew something she didn't. No matter. She had a few surprises of her own that he would have to finagle.

"You seem pretty happy," he commented.

"I am." She smiled up at him. "And I owe it all to you."

"I don't deserve you," he murmured softly before leaning closer to kiss her.

She sighed against him as she looked down at the ring on her finger. "You're stuck with me now."

"God, I hope so," he whispered against her hair.

Caydence looked up at him. "What's the matter?"

"Nothing. I must be tired."

"Pity," she pouted.

"Don't worry, I'm not *that* tired." He grinned at her, and the darkness seemed to leave his eyes before he nuzzled her nose with his own. His lips were so close to hers, yet he kept them just out of reach.

Caydence tried to kiss him, but he moved his lips away. Her breath caught in her throat as his hand moved beneath

146

the top of her dress and rubbed against her nipple. "Oh...
tease."

"Looks like I'm not the only one." He worked over the
tiny nubs long enough for them to perk up before he slid his
hand out.

Caydence looked down and saw her arousal was just
barely visible. Maybe she should have put her bra on. She
moved as if to retrieve it, but his hand pulled her back. "I just
need—"

"Leave it." His eyes had darkened.

"Obviously, anyone can see...." She blushed.

"Let them." He gave her a sexy grin.

"Oh...," Caydence sighed when his mouth finally touched
down on hers. His hand ran through her hair and pulled her
head back with just enough force to make her curl her toes in
her shoes. His mouth ran a hot trail of kisses down her neck.
When her breath was almost trapped in her throat, he pulled
away.

"Ready to go?" He lifted her hand to his mouth and kissed
it.

She narrowed her eyes on him. "I was...now I'm ready
to stay."

"Too bad." He grinned at her. "You're adorable when
you pout."

Caydence pulled her hand away from his. "Let's go."

Thankfully, Tyler gave her a little reprieve, which allowed
her headlights to no longer be visible to the outside world.
By the time they made it to the dinner table, she was back to
normal. She did feel a little self-conscious. Caydence had never

been this scandalous in her apparel before. So far, no one else seemed to notice but her, which was almost disappointing. Of course, the only person she wanted to notice was Tyler, and he seemed slightly pre-occupied.

As she was pushing her food around on her plate, Tyler leaned over to whisper in her ear. "What's the matter, Caydence?"

Her eyes met his and she pouted slightly. "Nothing."

There were two other couples at the table, but all of them seemed to be absorbed with the entertainment going on before them. A beautiful young woman was singing jazz with a small quartet. None of them noticed him nibbling at her ear lobe. Caydence gasped slightly, and coughed into her hand as if she were choking.

"You all right there, honey?" One of the older ladies asked her as she turned back to a sputtering Caydence.

"Something just went down the wrong way." Caydence waved her concern away. Thankfully, the lady's attention returned to the singer.

Tyler scooted his chair even closer to hers. He continued to eat his food as one hand caressed her leg. "Eat your food, Caydence."

A pulse beat in her ears as his hand moved further up her leg, pushing the hem of her skirt slightly. She took a bite of the potatoes in front of her, and tried to swallow them without choking as Tyler hand pushed her skirt up. She was incredibly thankful that the tablecloth blocked anyone else's view, especially when his hand found its way to the top of her thigh.

He leaned over and whispered in her ear, "*Tease.*"

Caydence turned around and looked at him challengingly, as if to ask, what are you going to do about it? He kissed her cheek and moved back to whisper in her ear again. "*Don't move, Caydence.*"

What in the world was he about to...? Oh...that. Caydence stiffened slightly as his hand moved between her legs.

"*Open for me.*" His breath was hot on her ears.

Caydence was suddenly glad that they were the table at the back of the room closest to the exit, or the others might have gotten quite a show. Especially when his finger rubbed against her clit. She turned to look at him and saw the wicked grin on his face. Turning away, she moved her fork across her plate and tried to take another bite, but all she could think about was the gentle hum he was creating in her body. She could feel her face flushing as his fingers stroked her slowly, so slow no one else noticed the movement.

He leaned over to her. "*Don't even think about finishing.*"

Her eyes flew to his. So not only was she no more than two feet from the rest of the table, trying her best not to show any sign of what they were doing, he was also telling her she could not have an orgasm, even if it came under those circumstances. Caydence squeezed her bottom together, trying to contain the desire that was starting to race through her. When he felt her flinch against his fingers, he stopped moving.

Caydence closed her eyes and tried to still the aching throb inside, maintain as much control as she could over her traitorous body. She reached for her wine glass and almost knocked it over when his fingers started to move again. Her insides were like liquid fire, and her breasts rose to the challenge as her nipples strained against her dress. Tyler definitely noticed, for his eyes were trained to them.

His fingers moved faster against her traitorous body, and Caydence found the desire climbing dangerously inside her. She was wet for him, and bit her mouth to keep from calling out his name. His rules were torturous, and he knew it. Caydence could only follow them for so long, and was about to let go when he moved his hand away and pulled her dress back down her leg.

Caydence held her napkin up to her face, trying to hide the way her lips trembled with desire for him. Closing her eyes, she tried to settle the swirling emotions inside her. She had never wanted any man the way she wanted him. When he leaned over, she looked at him from heavy lidded eyes.

His eyes flashed and he put his napkin on his plate. "I'm not very hungry."

She gave him a half smile. "That's too bad. I'm starving."

"I think it's time to take this show on the road," he muttered softly as he caught her innuendo. He held his hand out to her and she took it.

Caydence couldn't agree more. As they walked down the hallway, she almost didn't trust her legs to work. Every step she took, the more she felt like she was in a trance. He was the Pied Piper, leading her to something wicked and delicious. Her mind turned over one scenario after the other, keeping her in a state of attraction that was deliciously painful.

When they entered the elevator, she moved to the back.

He stepped closer to her, like a man who was starving. His lips were on hers before she could take a breath. Tyler yanked her closer to his body, and the force of his embrace only served as more fuel to her fire. She glanced up and saw the small camera that was recording every second. A wicked smile crossed her face as she wondered how many couples had been recorded in the same state. When the elevator dinged, she didn't want him to move away, but they were on their floor.

The walk to the room seemed like it took an eternity. She was so hot and ready for him Caydence wasn't entirely sure she wouldn't let him take her right there on the hallway floor, other people be damned. He had a pull over her she could not understand. She was infinitely appreciative that the universe had put him in her path. If Dalton had never broken her heart, she wouldn't be right here with the most amazing creature she had ever met. The best part was, it didn't have to end the minute they stepped off the boat.

As he opened the door, she felt her heart skip a beat and forced herself to walk calmly into the room. Caydence stood transfixed in her spot as he closed the door and locked it. His steps toward her were slow, and almost punctuated with the way his eyes seemed to devour every inch of her. When he finally stopped before her, he kissed her harder than he ever had before. Caydence met the forceful thrust of his tongue with her own. She was a woman in the wild throes of desire, desirable, hot, and ready.

His fingers stroked the outside of her dress, rubbing the fabric against her nipples that wanted to feel so much more than the material covering them. His hands pulled the top of the dress down and squeezed them tight. Breaking the kiss, his mouth devoured the skin at her neck, until he made his way down to her breasts that seemed to arch toward him enticingly. He squeezed them in his hands as his tongue licked against them.

"Oh!" Caydence felt her insides tighten as he sucked her nipple into his mouth and bit it gently in his teeth.

"God, I want you," he whispered when he finally released her.

Caydence whimpered in response. She had been well past longing for him hours ago. Now she was desperate for him. She reached down and unzipped his pants. When her hands wrapped around his cock, he bucked against her. Before she knew it, she found herself up against the wall.

Tyler shoved her skirt up and lifted her off the floor, and she wrapped her legs around him. When he slid inside her, she almost lost her mind. Tyler bit her shoulder and started to pump into her. Caydence was already dripping around him.

"Yes…you feel so good." He nibbled her ear and she nearly lost her mind. "Hold on tight, Caydence."

She didn't plan on letting him go any time soon. They were connected in ways she could never fully explain. As he slammed into her over and over again, the rising pitch was a painful bliss that she wanted to ride for eternity. A fire started inside her, and started to flow through the rest of her as the first orgasm ripped through her. "Tyler!"

"God yes, say my name baby. Oh." He bit her neck and Caydence nearly lost her mind all over again.

"*Tyler!*" The force behind her next orgasm made her shout

his name.

Caydence was trapped in a cyclone of desire that could topple the strongest woman. She held on as he continued to work his magic on her. Her hips gyrated against his, riding the length of him the best that she could in this position. When he jerked against her, she knew he had finally found his finish.

She laid her head against his shoulder as he carried her to the bed. Lowering her, he kissed her eyelids and nuzzled her nose with his own. She sighed. "You're some kind of wonderful. Tyler."

"You're my inspiration." His mouth fell over hers, and every inch of her body relaxed against him.

Her eyelids fluttered up and down. A hazy dreamlike state filled her, and she heard him chuckle as he spoke into her ear. "Sleep now, Caydence. You're going to need your rest for tomorrow."

Chapter 18

When Caydence woke up, she found that Tyler was gone again. Where in the world could he be? It was early in the morning—that she knew for sure, as the sun barely poured into their window. A tray of food was sitting on the bed next to her, and Caydence smiled. How thoughtful. She nibbled on some of the fruit, and smirked when she saw a handful of bacon on the tray. A man after her own heart, for sure.

When she got up and walked to the bathroom, she saw a white dress hanging from the shower with a note attached to it. *Wear this.* Caydence ran a finger against the soft fabric and smiled. Simple and beautiful, delicate like a white rose. Tyler had impeccable taste. What a wonderful surprise, as long as he didn't think he could plan her entire wardrobe. "He's not Dalton," she reminded herself.

Caydence moved the dress so that she could take a quick shower. When she was done, she dried her hair and put on a little makeup to try to hide some of the rings under her eyes. Caydence had not slept very well. Last night, the winds had been stronger than other nights. It had kept her awake, and while she would have loved to spend the night making love to Tyler, he was fast asleep throughout all of it. She shivered as she thought of the irrational fears that had raced through her head, like how cruel it would be to sink in the middle of the ocean now that she had found Mr. Right.

She eyed the dress, wondering what they were doing today that required dressing up. The boat had docked near the islands late yesterday afternoon. Maybe they were going to explore the islands. She tried not to overthink it as she slid the dress over her head. The fabric swished around her and she sighed. Twirling around in a circle, she was reminded of how she had spun around for hours at a time in the beautiful dresses her father had treated her to on occasion. Life had been so much more carefree back then.

Looking in her bag, she retrieved the one necklace she took with her everywhere. It had been a gift from her grandparents and her father for her sweet sixteen birthday. For some reason, it just seemed appropriate. Pushing her hair back on one side, she added a clip to keep it out of her face. Glancing in the mirror, she was happy with the effects. She almost looked ethereal, like a nymph ready for her lover.

As if on cue, the door opened. As Tyler looked over at her, she did a small spin. "How do I look?"

"Stunning." His eyes held meaning she could not understand. He held a small bouquet of flowers in his hands. "Are you ready?"

"Where are we going?" She asked him curiously as she walked over to him. He was a little more dressed up than usual himself. He was wearing khakis with a white button up long sleeved shirt. She was half tempted to undo the buttons and run her hands over his chest, but Caydence controlled that impulse.

"These are for you." He handed the flowers to her and kissed her on the cheek.

"What a beautiful color," exclaimed Caydence. She had never seen the color before. It was somewhere between a pink and orange, almost like color of the sun as it moved just above the water's edge.

"They remind me of how you look when you blush."

Caydence felt the heat rise in her cheeks when her eyes met his. "I don't think I've ever blushed so much in my life."

His lips met hers and he whispered against them. "You look ravishing."

Her heart skipped in her chest. "As much as I would like to be ravished...I think I'm more curious about what you have planned for today."

"I'm not telling," he teased her.

"I figured as much."

"As adorable as that pout is, you'll just have to wait." He winked at her. "It's a surprise."

"Ooh. I love surprises." Caydence gave him a bright smile.

"I hope so," he almost whispered.

Caydence held his hand as he navigated through the halls. Were they going dancing? That could be fun...a little awkward considering she had never taken lessons before, but she would manage if he was there with her. As they walked well past the dance studio, she tried to think about what else they could be doing. When he led her to the path leading them off the boat, she looked up at him. "Are we exploring the island?"

"Perhaps," he answered with a soft smile.

"This might not be the right attire." She smoothed out the skirt that was ruffling around her legs.

"You're dressed appropriately." He kissed her on the cheek.

"If you say so."

Caydence leaned her head on his shoulder as they walked down the plank leading them to the dock. Tyler pulled her to the right, leading her onto the beach. She was thankful that she had paired her dress with a simple pair of sandals. Trying to walk in the sand on heels would have been a mistake. Her eyes were everywhere at once, trying to figure out what they were doing. The blue skies, the white sand, the ocean waves that rippled softly onto the shore. The further they walked, the more curious she became.

When they reached a small secluded area, he stopped. There was a small white arch with white curtains swaying in the breeze. Alice and George stood beside it, and a woman in a flowing robe stood in front of it. To Caydence, it looked like someone was getting married. She smiled. "Are we going to a wedding?"

Tyler lifted her hand to his mouth and kissed it gently. "If you'll have me."

"Wait, what?"

"I'm asking you to marry me. Right here, right now."

Caydence looked in his eyes and saw he was being

157

absolutely serious. "This is what you've been doing?"

"Yes. Guilty as charged." He put a hand on her face. "You never answered...."

Caydence closed her eyes, not because she wanted to say no, but because tears were starting to gather in her eyes. This had to be one of the most impulsively romantic things ever. "Tyler...." His eyes became guarded as he waited for her to answer, and Caydence realized he was just as vulnerable as she was. She put her hand on his cheek and smiled softly. "I will."

He kissed the underside of her hand, and Caydence closed her eyes. His mouth came down to hers, and she put her hand up before he could kiss her. "Ah-ah...it's not time for that yet."

"Then let's get to it."

Caydence walked down the beach arm in arm with him. Tears fell down her face, and she tried to wipe them away with her free hand. She was going to be a blubbery mess before long. Her eyes met Tyler's when they stopped before the arch.

"Oh, here sweetheart, here's a tissue." Alice handed her a tissue.

Caydence blushed. "You both were in on this too?"

"Tyler confessed the truth to us and asked us to help him with this surprise," George answered with a rueful smile.

"You sure make a beautiful bride," squealed Alice.

"Yes, she does," Tyler added.

"Let me hold those for you, dear girl," Alice offered.

She was loathe to do so, for the flowers were so beautiful,

but she handed them over. Caydence felt a rosy glow fill her, and for once didn't care if the rest of the world saw her blushing. She had the look of a woman who was well loved from head to toe, and she was basking in it. As the minutes ticked by, she memorized every detail in her mind. The water roared nearby, as the frothy white waves crashed over the clear blue waters. Her dress brushed against her legs as the breeze blew against her. A few birds called overhead, as if congratulating them in a fly by. Throughout it all, Tyler's eyes never left her face, as if he were memorizing every centimeter of her smile.

When the woman asked if he had the ring, Caydence remembered the plastic ring that she had left on the counter in the room. She was suddenly wishing she had brought it with her, but to her surprise, Tyler was more than prepared.

"Right here." He took her hand and slid a ring on her finger.

Caydence almost cried. How could he understand her so well? The band was simple — white gold with small diamonds embedded into it. Simple, sweet, perfect. She nibbled her lip, mostly because she was afraid to look up at him. If she did, she was liable to lose control of her emotions. Even though she tried to stall the tears that wanted to fall, she could not. His hand brushed them away and pulled her chin up slightly so her eyes met his.

"Do you like it?"

"It's perfect," she whispered. Just like him, she wanted to add, but she was afraid no other words would come out. "I don't have one for you."

"We can take care of that later." He turned to the woman. "Please continue."

When the officiant finally proclaimed that it was time to kiss the bride, Tyler pulled her close to him. His kiss was tender, as if his lips were able to speak clearer than any words he could utter at that moment in time. Caydence felt her heart swell inside her. His arms wrapped around her and he lifted her up. Tyler spun her in his arms once and lowered her to the ground, where she put her head against his chest.

Maybe fairytales did exist, she thought to herself. She heard a sniffle behind her, and turned to see Alice crying. Caydence smiled at her as Alice handed her flowers back. Caydence knew this would be one of the most beautiful moments of her life.

"Any regrets?" Tyler asked her.

"No photographer," she pouted.

Tyler smiled and pointed behind them. There had been someone taping it all along.

"How in the world did you manage this?" she wondered aloud.

"A lot of help. Turns out, the ship is filled with hopeless romantics." He winked at her.

"Well, I guess it's a good thing it was a couple's cruise." She was surprised to see that Alice and George were already walking away from the ceremony, as if they were giving them privacy. Yes, he had planned every single detail, and he hadn't hired a planner to do it. Tyler was a miracle worker.

"Care to take a walk, Mrs. Jensen?"

She shivered when his hand ran along her spine. "Say

that again."

"*Mrs....*"

Wrapping her arms around his neck, she pulled him down to a kiss that took her breath away. "I love you," she whispered.

"Good...don't you forget it." His golden eyes were clouded for just a moment before he released her.

He reached for her hand, and Caydence felt his fingers tickle the bottom of her hand as they walked down the beach. She was relieved that this was the secret he was keeping from her. He had been brooding just a little over the past few days, but she hadn't delved deeper.

"That means I'm actually on my honeymoon."

"Sure does." He winked at her. "Is it everything you hoped it would be?"

"That depends on what you have planned for later," she teased him.

"You'll just have to wait."

A wave of water washed over her feet, and Caydence giggled as she fell into him. He caught her at the last minute, and the two of them toppled to the ground. They were both laughing uncontrollably as the next wave of water rushed around them. When she leaned down to kiss him, Tyler wrapped his hands in her hair and pulled her closer. Neither one of them noticed the passage of time, nor how drenched their clothing had become. They were both lost in the bliss of the moment.

Chapter 19

By the time they returned to the cabin, Caydence wasn't sure that her day could get any better. She couldn't have planned a better wedding. Intimate, memorable. Simple and absolutely breathtaking. No one had ever made her feel so truly loved.

"Oh, look!" squealed Caydence. The bed was sprinkled in rose petals in the shape of a heart. Faux candles flickered from different places. Caydence looked up at him. "You had them do this too?"

"Guilty as charged."

"What if I had said no?" She smirked at him.

"I don't know...." His eyes looked slightly troubled.

Walking over to him, she put her lips against his. "Thank you."

"For?"

"Making this day the day I always dreamt it would be." Tears filled her eyes and she looked away from him.

"The day isn't over yet, dear *wife*."

Wife. Her heart skipped a beat. To have and hold...to

cherish. She wasn't sure she could handle much more. "What comes next?"

"I imagine the same that happens on most wedding nights," he grinned.

"Oh…. Well, I guess we could do that. If you wanted to, that is."

"Don't get shy on me now, Mrs. Jensen." A knock sounded on the door. "Right on time."

"What is that?"

"Dessert." His wicked smile told her that he was definitely up to something.

Caydence went to sit on the edge of the bed and found a small box on the floor. It was tied with a large red bow. "What's this?"

"Open it." His eyes twinkled mischievously.

"Tyler, you've already given me so much. I don't have anything for you."

"You are all I need," he said as he carried a tray over to the bed. "Now, open it."

"Fine." She toyed with the bow for a second before untying it. Removing the red tissue paper inside, she found a beautiful white lace lingerie set. It was delicate, something she would have picked out for herself for her wedding day. "This is beautiful."

"Like you." He leaned over and kissed her on the shoulder.

"I just don't understand all this." She gestured to the bed, the food, the dress, the ring. "How can you know so much about me?"

"The truth?" His mouth turned into a grin.

"Yes."

"I may have had a little help." He gestured to the phone that was sitting on the small coffee table.

"How did you get her to help you?"

"She's really a romantic at heart, if you get past the slightly foul language."

Caydence giggled. "Janelle does have a potty mouth sometimes, but it's usually cat induced."

His eyebrow rose curiously. "I'm trying to figure out if that was a double entendre or not."

"Nope. She's got two cats that are always climbing the walls, driving her nuts."

"That explains the screech I heard followed by a loud hiss."

"A crash then a boom?"

"Yep."

Caydence giggled. "That happens a lot when she's on the phone. All the other times they want nothing to do with her. The minute she gets on the phone—well, all hell breaks loose."

"I see." He fingered the lingerie. "So, are you going to try it on?"

Caydence bit her bottom lip. "All right, but you can't look. Otherwise, the surprise will be ruined."

He crossed his hands over his heart and held his hand up in front of him. Then he turned around and faced the other direction. Caydence did not waste any time taking her clothes off. She dropped them in a pile on the floor. When his shoulders bunched in reflex, she knew he realized that she was completely naked behind him. The top of the lingerie was more like a baby doll dress. The lacey cups were not as sheer as the material that ruffled from it. Under the top, she now wore a lace thong that left her cheeks exposed. He would have to be a blind man not to appreciate the way it fit her body. With her curves, there was very little left to the imagination.

"Okay...."

Tyler turned so slowly, she wasn't entirely sure he had moved at all. When he looked her over, she saw him clench his mouth shut. His cheeks seemed rigid.

Caydence pouted. "You don't like it?"

"No. I like it almost too much. Come here, wife." He held his hand out to her.

Caydence almost tiptoed over to him. It was then that she saw the tray of goodies. "Strawberries?"

"With chocolate and whipped cream." He grinned at her.

"Oh...that's all?" Caydence almost expected some extreme delicacies. These were things that she could have any time.

"You've never had strawberries like this before." He swirled one in whipped cream and put it in his lips. His crooked his finger at her, waving her toward him.

At first, Caydence wasn't sure what he wanted her to do, so she moved closer and licked the whipped cream off the strawberry before taking a bite. One bite, then another, until there was no barrier between their lips. When he licked the whipped cream from her mouth, she realized that it was not really about the strawberries at all.

"Mmmm...delicious," he murmured as his lips moved

over hers.

When his tongue slid into her mouth, Caydence sighed. "That was delicious."

"There's more where that came from. Lay down."

"Oh?" Caydence was curious, but she did as he asked and lay back against the pillow.

Tyler pushed the flowing top away to expose her belly. Sprinkling some of the chocolate over her belly, his tongue lapped against her skin. Her flesh crawled under his mouth, the gentle touch mixed with a promise of what was yet to come. She curled her toes when his teeth nibbled her flesh. He spent the next lifetime on the bottom half of her body, being especially careful not to get the food on her new lingerie. Mixing her flesh with fruity sweetness, it was as if he were devouring every inch of her, and Caydence felt delicious.

When he spread her legs and took a finger of cream, Caydence whimpered in anticipation. Her eyes met his, and she could see the gentle danger inside them. He was working himself up, and she knew it. Tyler placed the cream on her and started to lick it off. Caydence writhed beneath him as he sucked it off her clit. He repeated this process so many times she thought she was going to lose her mind. When his tongue slid inside her, Caydence shook beneath him.

"Mmmmm...there's the cream I like."

Caydence shook against his encouraging words as she rode his face. The whole world seemed to be spiraling out of control. She sighed in contentment when the orgasm was over. He rained kisses up and down her legs, nibbling every few inches. Her toes flicked in reflex when he settled on her ankles. She almost expected him to devour her feet, but what he did was even more enjoyable. His hands massaged the arches, working out any of the knots that had formed in them. She was instantly relaxed and feeling like the luckiest woman in the world as his hands worked up her calves to her thighs. When they slid under her bottom and started to massage her cheeks, she whimpered softly.

"What's wrong, baby?"

"You're too good to be true." She smiled at him and licked her lips.

His eyes were drawn to her mouth. His hands roamed up her body and played with her nipples that were stretched tight against the lace. "I'm real, Caydence. And I have a lifetime to prove my love for you."

She winced when his teeth sank into her stomach. He was fire and ice. The push and pull of every gravitational force. When he moved up and lowered the top, exposing just one of her breasts, Caydence shivered in anticipation.

He drizzled chocolate over it and licked his lips. "That's quite a delectable cherry you've got there."

Caydence looked down at her breasts and grinned. "You're not going to eat that, are—? Oh...."

His actions clearly answered that question, as he licked the chocolate away from her nipple. He sucked her hard into his mouth and bit her gently. When the chocolate was all gone, he added more, murmuring, "I've got quite the sweet tooth."

"It would appear you do, Mr. Jensen," she teased him.

Before long they were out of chocolate sauce, but that didn't seem to matter to Tyler as he pleasured her over and over. Caydence was near her limit of what she could handle, as her lids drifted open and shut. He had made love to almost every inch of her with his hands and lips. When he finally plunged inside of her, she felt a liquid fire rise up inside her. The soft gentle motion stoked the flames as her silky wet core wrapped around his heat.

"God, you feel so good." Tyler slid in and out. He leaned over and suckled her breast as he continued to plunge into her depths. She shivered around him in response. Tyler slid a hand between them and stroked her clit as he took every inch of her. Caydence was fully mastered by his prowess as the lights exploded around her eyes.

As the orgasm pushed her forward, Caydence felt like she was floating on a delicious cloud that soared higher and higher, pushed by torturous lovemaking. She had no idea how long they continued, but her juices were starting to dry up and a slight friction created a new sensation.

"What's this, all out of cream, Caydence?"

She flinched slightly as he slid in and out of her. Her insides still gripped him tight, but where there was a soft heat, there was a dangerous fire as the rawness of the moment tickled her senses, the same rawness that was driving Tyler to the brink. She could tell he was close to his release, but he was trying to hold himself back, enjoy every moment.

"So tight and hot...mmmm...." Tyler was fighting for control, but when Caydence wrapped her legs around him and pulled him in tighter, he forgot all reason as he started to ride her like a man possessed with desire. When he came inside her, she quivered around him one last time.

"That was…." He tried to come up with a description as he panted above her.

"Delicious?" suggested Caydence. She winced slightly as he pulled out of her. She was a little sore, but it was worth every minute of it.

"Did I hurt you?" he asked with concern.

"A little…but pain is pleasure sometimes. No regrets." She brought his head down to hers and kissed him softly on the mouth.

"Good, Mrs. Jensen." He scooped her up in his arms and carried her from the bed to the shower.

"What are you doing?" she whispered.

"Taking care of my wife. You're a little sticky." He grinned as he removed her top and tossed it on the floor.

"Tyler…." She knew this could lead to more sex, and as hot as it was, she wasn't sure her body could handle any more tonight.

"Relax, Caydence. I'm not going to ravish you. Trust me." He nuzzled her nose with his and kissed her softly on the lips. He turned on the water and checked the temperature, before helping her into the hot streaming water behind her.

He spent the next few moments cleaning her with a tenderness that brought tears to her eyes. She closed her eyes and let herself relive the entire day in her head. Caydence almost felt like she was living in a fairy tale, where the prince rescued her from her life. In this instance, she was being given a second chance for happiness in a world that had always seemed to elude her. Tomorrow, they would have to talk about that future in more depth. There were so many things they would need to discuss.

After Tyler finished and toweled her off gently, he carried her back to the bed and lay her down softly. When he climbed in beside her, she snuggled into his warmth. She was starting to love sleeping naked against him. Caydence sighed as she drifted to sleep next to him.

Chapter 20

The next few days passed so quickly that Caydence was struggling to deal with the cruise coming to an end. This whole time, the two of them had fallen under some kind of romantic spell. Sometimes she woke up feeling like it was all just a dream—the most delicious one she had ever had, but still completely unbelievable. If this was a dream, it was one she never wanted to wake up from. She knew they would have battles along the way. No relationship was perfect, and with this one being so new, it was fragile. They would have to cultivate it from the bottom up.

They had talked about the future, and planned for Caydence to move into Tyler's house. She would either sell hers or lease it to someone for income. When they returned to port, they would take the first plane back to Livingston. Caydence was going to retrieve her car and follow him to his house. She was actually pretty curious about what kind of place Tyler lived in. Would it look like a bachelor pad? She imagined it was kept pretty clean considering how much work he was constantly doing. She had even caught him working a few times this past week. Caydence had let it slide, because she knew the nature of his work required him to check the markets from time to time. Stocks didn't stay level just because he decided to take a vacation.

Rubbing her temples, Caydence realized that maybe she'd had too much to drink the night before. They had done a mixology class, which had been more than worth it considering how frisky it had made her feel. Reckless and carefree, two feelings she was coming to terms with whenever she was around her husband. *Husband.* She still had trouble believing he belonged to her. She looked down at her ring and sighed. He was so much more than she'd ever dreamed of. Would he ever have second thoughts? Would he regret taking such a leap with her? What if they returned to reality and he realized that he had made a big mistake? It was her greatest fear.

Now that she had him, Caydence just could not think of what life would be like without him. The thought brought tears to her eyes within seconds. She had never felt like she couldn't live without any other man in her life. Caydence loved him — rationally, irrationally, either way the feelings were tattooed straight to her soul, as if she had always been looking for him. Speaking of looking for him…where was he?

As if on cue, the door opened. He closed it behind him and smiled at her. "Good morning. How are you feeling?

Caydence blushed as she remembered how much of the night before had been spent. Having drunk far too much, she'd spent a significant amount of time making friends with the toilet. He was there with her, rubbing her back and holding her hair out of her face. "My head hurts."

"I thought it might, so I brought you this." He handed her a bottle of ibuprofen and a large bottle of water.

Caydence gave him a thankful smile. "You're some kind of wonderful."

"I paid for them to send the bags on to the house, so we don't have to retrieve them at the airport." His voice was soft, as if he knew loud tones would grate on her nerves.

"They can do that?"

"Yep." He grinned.

"Then I just have to pick up my car." She snuggled against him when he lay down next to her.

"Don't get too comfortable. We dock soon."

"Already?" Caydence closed her eyes and felt reality crashing down around her. What would happen next? Reality was so close that she wanted to keep it at bay.

"Caydence, relax. It's all going to be fine." He kissed the top of her head.

"You say that now, but here, it's just us. Nothing else to get in the way. There, I have to learn how to share you with the rest of the world." Caydence was not looking forward to that.

Tyler stroked her cheek. "I'm all yours, Caydence. Only yours."

She looked up at his eyes and saw something hidden beneath. "What's wrong, Tyler?"

"Nothing. We should get ready." He kissed her softly and went to make sure his bags were set.

Caydence sat up and stretched. She went to do her

morning toiletries, and then joined him in packing up the rest of her things. When they were done, the first whistle could be heard. "Guess it's time to go?"

"Sounds that way." He smiled and gathered her in his arms. "Nothing's going to change, Caydence."

He said that now, but Caydence knew that life could change in the blink of an eye. Take this cruise, for instance. She had entered it hell bent on staying single for the rest of her life. In the long run, she had fallen madly in love with the handsome stranger who had followed her halfway across the world. Their love was new, fragile if held under a microscope. She fought against dissecting it piece by piece. If logic came in at this moment in time, it might destroy her. She closed her eyes and blocked it out the best that she could.

Tyler lifted her head up to look in her eyes. "Breathe, Caydence."

She took a soft breath and sighed against him when he brought his lips down to hers. If every day started with his gentle kiss, she could face any demons, even the ones that only existed in her own mind. When the horn blasted again, she opened her eyes. "We really do need to go."

"Yes, we do. You ready?"

"The bags?"

"They will have them delivered to us. Promise."

"Okay." Caydence moved toward the door, then turned around and took one last look at the room she would remember for the rest of her life. Her eyes started to tear up.

"Don't look so sad, Caydence. We've got a lifetime of memories to make."

"I know," she whispered as she reached for his hand.

They had each come on this boat for their own reasons. Alone. Not knowing that their worlds would completely collide in such a way. Now, they left hand in hand prepared to move forward to the next stage of their relationship. Whatever that brought, Caydence was prepared to stand by his side.

Before she knew it, they were already in the ride that would bring them back to the airport. She lay her head on his shoulder and smiled. "So, tell me about your family again."

"My brother is an attorney. If you think I work hard, you should see him. He's pale, like a vampire. I don't think he ever sees the sun."

Caydence giggled. "Thomas?"

"Yes. Never did like to be called Tommie. I still call him that on occasion."

"Brute," she teased him.

"He's a pushover," he countered, pretending he misinterpreted her words.

"And your sister?"

"Which one? Abigail?"

"Yes." Abigail…that was the one who was still at home, she thought.

"Sixteen and spoiled rotten."

Caydence smiled as she thought about what having a sister might actually be like. Would they be good friends? "I bet she adores you."

"That's up for interpretation."

"And Janice?" Caydence asked him.

"She's twenty-six and has two kids. Happily married to

her high school sweetheart, Ollie."

Caydence snuggled against him. "You have two nieces?"

"Yes, Anna and Lucy." He smiled despite himself. "Cutest little princesses you'll ever meet."

Tears fell down her face and she wiped them away, hoping he wouldn't notice, but he did.

"What's wrong, Caydence?"

"I hope they like me."

"They will love you, Caydence."

"I never had siblings before. And well, I have no one." Caydence didn't know how to tell him how she was feeling. He was giving her the family she hadn't realized she missed until this moment, when she thought about the only family she had—none. Her father, her grandparents, they were all gone. Would his family welcome her, the way that hers would have welcomed him? Or would they be upset with his impulsive move? She wasn't even sure if they knew yet.

"You have me, Caydence. And you'll have them too."

"Will your mom be mad?"

"Probably." He sighed and ran a hand through his hair.

Caydence closed her eyes. "Maybe we should have waited."

"She'll get over it. Especially when she sees how happy you've made me." He kissed her softly on the lips, and Caydence sighed against him.

"I'm not sure who got the better deal here. I've managed to find the sexiest man alive, and gained a whole new family to fall in love with too."

He brought his mouth down to her ear and whispered

into it. "Yes, but I have the most insatiable creature that I get to spend a lifetime pleasing."

Caydence shivered as his words sunk in. A lifetime of pleasure. She liked the sound of that. So did her body, which was already waking up at the mere thought of him ravishing her. She started wondering what it would be like to join the mile high club, but knew just thinking about him all day would make the wait worthwhile.

"And how often do you see your family?"

"As often as work allows. They all live nearby," he grinned.

"Nearby?" Really...she wasn't sure how she felt about that. Would his mother be overbearing like other mothers-in-law? What about his father? He barely mentioned him.

"Well, an hour away, if you consider that near."

"Your father?"

"Also an attorney. He works for the state foster system, representing parents who are trying to adopt foster kids permanently. He's brought quite a few families together."

"Oh, wow. Sounds like you got your workaholic nature from him." She winked at him.

"And my impulsive nature. You know, he convinced my mom to elope with him when she was eighteen. They had just graduated from high school."

"So, your dad will probably forgive you before your mother?"

"Well, Mom will come around. She's still mad at my ex, so she's a little protective."

Caydence nodded as if she understood, but she didn't.

Not really. Tyler rarely spoke of what happened between him and his ex. He had alluded to the fact that she had cheated on him, but that was about it. Of course, that was really all she had needed to know, because Caydence knew what it was like to find out someone who she loved had been sneaking around behind her back.

"Looks like we're here. You ready?"

"Yep." Her heart skipped a beat. Just a few more hours and Caydence would be able to lose herself in his arms again.

Chapter 21

The day passed almost excruciatingly slowly, from the long wait in the airport, to the drive that seemed to take forever. In reality, it had only been a few hours, but Caydence was nervous with anticipation. Every moment, she wondered what would happen next. Her life had been a whirlwind over the past few weeks, an adventure she hadn't realized she needed. She prayed that every day would be that way with him, that they would love each other just as much as they did right now.

As their cars pulled into a long paved drive, Caydence nearly stopped breathing. There were clearly some things she still did not know about Tyler, for as she looked up she saw a large three story brick house with white pillars in front of it. Was that a mansion? It certainly looked large enough to qualify. The lawn was well manicured, and trees outlined the entire drive as she drove past them. When she parked her car, she sat there in the silence for a moment, gathering her wits about her.

When Tyler opened her door, she looked up at him. "I

179

think there's still a lot to tell me."

"I'm *very* good at my job," he chuckled.

"Uhm…seriously?" Her eyes felt huge, for she was taking in everything around her.

"Come on, let me show you around."

"In one day?" she teased him.

"It's not that big."

"Liar!" she teased him, and punched him playfully on the arm as she got out of her car.

His mouth came down on hers and he plunged his tongue into her depths. By the time he pulled back, both of them were taking in ragged breaths. "I've been thinking about doing that all day."

"Oh?" She licked her lips. "What else have you been thinking about?"

"That, you'll have to find out." He walked her over to the steps leading up to the large white double doors. He unlocked the door and pushed it open. "But first…."

When he swept her up in his arms, Caydence squeaked. "What are you doing?"

"Carrying my wife over the threshold. It's good luck."

"Oh. Well, carry on then." Caydence would take any luck they could get at this point. She wanted nothing but good luck to lead them for the rest of their lives.

When he stepped through the doorway, she thought he would let her back down, but he continued to hold her in his arms. His mouth touched against hers and she sighed as he kissed her passionately. She was ready to be lost in the moment when a voice interrupted them.

"Who the hell is she?" A woman's shrill voice interrupted the silence.

Caydence was taken aback. Why was there a woman in Tyler's house? When he set her down, Caydence saw that Tyler was just as confused. Not knowing exactly what was going on, she stepped in front of him as if to protect him from the angry stare down that was coming from the beautiful blonde standing in front of them.

"I'm his *wife*. And you?"

"Wife?" The woman sniffed in irritation at her. "I'm his fiancée."

Caydence's breath caught in her throat. She turned to look up at Tyler, and saw his features were haunted. "What's going on?"

"Olivia *was* my fiancée," his voice cut out tersely.

"So what, you followed this piece of ass to get back at me? I knew Dalton had sold his ticket. I never imagined the lengths you would take to get back at us."

"Us?" Caydence whispered. It was as if she knew the answer before he even opened his mouth.

"She doesn't know? Oh, this is rich. Dalton didn't know either, darling. Don't worry yourself too much over that." Olivia actually looked sorry for her.

"What is going on?"

"Your lovely *husband*," she said as if that world were a falsity. "Found out that I was sleeping with Dalton Mills. Tyler works with him from time to time, but not enough for either one of them to know the connection."

A bizarre love triangle was unfolding before her, and

181

Caydence felt it chipping away at her happiness one word after another. "Tyler...."

"He suckered Dalton out of his tickets just so he could get back at both of us." Olivia put the nail in the coffin.

Caydence closed her eyes and tried to fight the emotions that were stirring inside of her. When she looked up she saw the guilt written all over his face. "How could you?"

Tears fell, and she didn't even bother to stop them. He deserved to see it. Their fragile love wrinkled up between them like a wilted bouquet of promises that had been forged in lies. Looking away from him, her shoulders slumped in defeat. Every inch of happiness that had circled around inside her crashed to the floor. She turned away from him and headed out the door.

"Caydence, wait—"

"Let her go, Tyler."

Caydence didn't even bother to wait to hear any of the rest of his explanation. Some things now made sense to her. Caydence had always felt like he was holding something back from her. She had never expected it to be this bad. Her heart was so numb when she drove away that no tears fell. By the time she made it back to her condo, reality had finally set in.

"Why?" she whispered as she closed the door behind her. She slid against it and cradled her head in her hands as she curled up on a ball on the floor. All the tears she had cried for Dalton were nothing compared to the flood that poured out of her eyes. Loud wracking sobs filled the silence around her. She looked down at the ring he had placed on her finger so tenderly, and she could not bring herself to remove it, even though it was a painful reminder.

When a knock sounded on the door, she almost jumped. Opening the door, she saw Janelle standing there with a bucket of ice cream.

"Janelle?"

"Are you going to let me in or not?" She asked her.

"How did you...?"

"A little birdie told me he was jackass." Janelle held up the tub. "Rocky road"

"Fine, but I don't want to talk about it," she lied.

"Okay. I've got all night, though. The jackasses won't let me have my bed back anyway."

Caydence rolled her eyes. "Another possession?"

"Apparently, the little shits think I'm going to sleep on the floor. They won't even share a corner. Fuckers." Janelle walked past her and went to search down some bowls.

Yep. Definitely a potty mouth. Caydence smiled in spite of herself. Following her into the kitchen, Caydence pulled out chocolate syrup and whipped cream. A memory flickered past her conscious, and she dropped the bottle on the floor. She was an instant mess, crying and sobbing as she tried to clean up the mess.

"Whoa, whoa...it's just a little chocolate," Janelle tried to console her, but none of her words made a difference. Caydence was working herself into such a frenzy that Janelle almost had to shake her to get her attention. "Caydence Faith!"

Caydence blinked and looked at her. "I just...how could he?"

Janelle opened her arms and hugged Caydence tight. "I

know, honey. Men are assholes. That's why I prefer women. Present company excluded, of course."

Caydence sniffed. "I traded one misery for another."

"Yes, but you were never *this* upset with Dalton," Janelle pointed out.

Caydence looked at the syrup staining the floor and started crying all over again. Love. Bliss. All shattered and broken on the floor. Anger was replaced with a numb void that she could not quite climb out of. Janelle sat there trying to get her attention, but Caydence just sat there holding the syrup bottle tight to her chest. She heard Janelle talking to someone in her haze.

"I don't know, Tyler. Anger I could understand. You fucked up, asshole. But this doesn't make sense." There was a pause. "She's sitting on the floor with death grip on a chocolate syrup bottle. Not quite sure what that means. Well, she dropped it on the floor, and the next thing I know she was an emotional wreck."

Emotional wreck? Was that what she was? Probably. Broken. Definitely. Caydence wasn't sure what she was supposed to do now. There had been too much heartache too fast. She remembered how beautiful Olivia was. Like a fourteen on a ten scale. To think that he could have had that, instead of her. And clearly, the woman still wanted him. What had seemed to be a bitter-ex trying to screw with a new relationship had quickly turned into purgatory for Caydence. He never denied the fact that he had purposefully snuck into her life, intent on seducing her to get back at Dalton. Was she just a pawn? She had been nothing but honest with him about her ex and how he had played her.

And as mad as that made her, what obliterated her was the fact that he had truly seemed to love her. But which words were true? Caydence wasn't sure it really mattered at this point. How could she even face him again, knowing what he'd done?

"Oh, well, that kind of explains it." Another pause. "Yes. I think so too."

Caydence was in such a state that she wasn't even sure anyone else existed outside her. She stared ahead, trapped in torturous memories that were so beautiful to her just hours ago. Now, she was numb as she tried to understand how her happiness could be stolen from her so fast. What had she done to deserve this?

She wasn't sure how long she had been sitting on the floor when she heard his voice. "Caydence...."

Tyler? The anger that had boiled inside her had left her feeling completely vacant. She didn't want to be here for the pain or the pleasure. Caydence was feeling broken and alone. Her eyes met his and she saw the sadness inside them. "Go away, Tyler."

"No." He refused. He tried to stroke her chin and she flinched.

When he got up and left, Caydence wanted to call for him to come back. Even though she was so angry with him, she knew she loved him. Part of her wanted to scream and shout at him, the other wanted him to fight for her. To tell her what she needed to hear. Anything that would make this right. Could he even make it right? She closed her eyes and fought against the wave of tears that wanted to crash down her face like the very waves that had crashed against them on the their wedding day. She tried to hold onto the anger, but she kept reliving the beauty, the love that had been so easy and carefree between them. Had it even been real?

She felt a wet cloth on her skin. Tyler was wiping the chocolate away from her in small tender strokes. Her eyes met his and a tear fell down her face. "Why are you here?"

"Because I love you, Caydence."

"You lied to me."

"Yes. No…. It's complicated." His eyes were pleading with her to listen to him.

"Then uncomplicate it," she challenged him. Caydence wanted him to convince her, to give her something to hold on to.

"I know it looks bad. It's all gotten twisted."

"Did you know he was my ex?"

"Yes." His voice was haunted

"You said that you saw me in the elevator."

"I did. I was going to confront him when I saw you."

"So he had no idea he was stuffing your fiancée?"

"No. He didn't. Not that he was all that selective."

Caydence winced. It was hard enough to know her ex had slept with his secretary. What Tyler was saying was that Dalton had slept with many more. That did not make Caydence feel any better. That Dalton had chosen all of those over her made her sick to her stomach even now. "Right."

Tyler ran a hand through his hair. "This is not going well."

"You think?" she said sarcastically.

"Caydence…."

"No…continue."

"I hoped you would be there."

"To seduce me. To ruin him. For what?"

"It wasn't like that." His eyes were tortured.

"You told me that you followed me there because you didn't want anyone to ever hurt me again. Was that even the truth."

"Yes, damn it!" His voice was almost shouting. "I love you, Caydence. I did NOT go there to manipulate you. I don't care how Olivia spun it. I know it sounds bad. I clearly did not think through how it would look."

"I don't know what to believe," Caydence whispered hollowly.

"Kiss me," he told her.

"No." She held her chin up.

"You owe me," he reminded her.

"What are you talking about? I *owe* you?" Caydence was ready to pummel him with her fists, and he wanted her to kiss him.

"I won it fair and square. A kiss. At an undisclosed time and place. Kiss me, Caydence. Or are you not a woman of your word?" His eyes met hers and Caydence glared at him.

"I don't think — "

"You promised." His words were almost a plea.

Caydence saw the grief building in his eyes. He was hurting too, but was that knowledge enough to erase the lies? She took a deep breath and leaned over to kiss him. The minute his lips touched hers, she felt the remorse, the love, the pain, the haunted soul that lay beneath the surface. He was a man who would throw himself at her feet, beg her for mercy if she was willing to give it. In one kiss he professed his love, and begged for her to feel the same. One kiss and he had said more than any man had ever said in her lifetime. When he broke it, she almost felt destroyed by it, the beauty behind it now lost on her.

Every memory passed through her head. The goofy grins, hand holding, ecstasy. The shoreline that had been the backdrop to the most romantic love story she had ever experienced, not even realizing she was living it herself. Tears fell down her face and she wanted to ask him to go, yet yearned more for him to stay with her forever, just like this — caught in a moment, where no matter what they fought over she would know his love was strong and true. He was her second chance, and the last one she ever wanted.

"Promise me."

"Anything," he answered without thinking.

"That you will kiss me like that every day for the rest of our lives."

Tears pooled in her eyes, and she smiled when she saw them in his own. She held a hand up to his cheek and caressed it softly.

"Always, my love." He pulled her into his arms and proved he was willing to do just that.

A small voice from the doorway interrupted them. "So are you going to introduce me, or should I just do that myself?"

Caydence broke the kiss and giggled. "Janelle, this is Tyler. My *husband*."

"Say that again," Tyler whispered.

"Husband."

"Get a room, you two!" teased Janelle.

"Well, this *is* my house, Janelle." Caydence wrinkled her nose at her.

"Oh, right. Got it. Nice to meet you—got to get back home before the shits burn down the house." Janelle grinned at them before she walked out of the room.

"She's something," grinned Tyler.

"Yes she is. Potty mouth and all."

"She knows you really well."

"Yeah, that was a risky move." She smiled. "Now, where were we?"

"Hmmm…about right here." Tyler brought his lips down to hers and she sighed against him. "I love you, Caydence."

"I love you more," she whispered.

His next kiss seemed to argue that point further, but they eventually came to the conclusion that their love for each other was equally matched. They had come together in a flurry of passion, the same passion that would build them up for years to come. Caydence knew they would meet each challenge head on, with a passion for each other that could light the stars in the sky with its brilliance.

Chapter 22

Almost three years later…

"Aunt Cadie!" a little voice squealed. A cherubic face came racing across the room.

"Lucy dear, be careful," Janice cautioned her four-year-old.

Caydence laughed and pulled the child up in her arms.

"Careful, love," Tyler whispered near her ear.

"I'm fine, Tyler. You all fuss so much." She smiled wryly at them. Resting Lucy on her hip, she snuggled near the little girl for a kiss.

"Aunt Cadie, you're big!"

"Lucy! That wasn't very nice."

Caydence giggled. "She's got a point, though."

Abigail pulled Lucy from her arms. "That's my nephew in there, be careful."

"Well, if you're taking her, then I'll take that one." Tyler's mom gestured to the one year old snuggled against Tyler's shoulder. The little girl saw her grandmother and squealed.

Tyler watched his child almost leap from his arms. "Traitor," he muttered.

Caydence smiled and kissed him on the cheek. "Well, *I* still love you."

"I'm thankful every day for that."

A sharp pain rippled over her belly and she gasped slightly. "You better be. This one thinks my bladder is a trampoline.

He placed his hand down and leaned over to reprimand the child growing inside her. "Be good to your mama, Jackson."

Her belly rolled at his voice and Caydence rolled her yes. "Every time."

The others had already slipped away, as Lucy was pulling them all into the other room to look at all the presents under the tree. Caydence followed them and looked at the family that had welcomed her with more than open arms. They had become so important to her, and she was thankful for every moment.

"Caydence, you have to come look at this," Abigail called her over excitedly.

"See, I told you she would love you," he reminded her.

Tears filled her eyes as she thought of everything she had gained. "I rather like having sisters."

"As long as you don't talk about me too much," he teased her.

"All the time." She winked at him and wrinkled her nose. "Sisters are awfully close—seems a pity. To not give Amelia a sister too."

"Good grief, woman, you weren't kidding about wanting a large family," he teased her.

"We can afford it. We've got plenty of love to spare." She rubbed her belly absently and looked around at the family that were all gathered around them. Aunts, uncles, cousins. The whole house was swarming with people. Caydence had never been happier.

About the Author

Ever since childhood, Elissa Daye has enjoyed reading stories as an escape from life. When she was a teenager she started to write her own stories that kept her entertained when she ran out of books to read. When she was accepted into Illinois Summer School for the Arts in her junior year of high school, she knew she wanted to become a writer. Elissa graduated from Illinois State University in December 1999 with a Bachelor of Science in Elementary Education, and began her teaching career, hoping to find moments to write in her free time. After seven years of teaching, Elissa decided to focus on her writing and made the decision to put her teaching years behind her so that she could create the stories she had always dreamed of. She is now happily married and a stay at home mom, who writes in every spare moment she can find, doing her best to master the art of multitasking to get everything accomplished.